Dear John

The Birthday Gift
Book 2

BETTY COLLIER

Afterword by Terry Gurley

A gripping redemption story fueled by Grace.

Contents

Introduction

This compelling sequel to *The Birthday Gift (Book 1)* picks up where the first book left the reader, engulfed in Grace Williams's heartfelt letter to her husband's despicable murderer. Rest assured this is not a spoiler alert as Bill Williams's death in Chapter 1 of the original story comes as no surprise. For new readers of this book series, don't think you missed something. The author grabs your attention from the get-go by including the letter from Grace in this book as Chapter 1. The letter itself brilliantly summarizes the original book from Grace's perspective. After you read it, don't be surprised if you have an inkling to stop and read Book 1 first, which can be found on Amazon here:
https://www.amazon.com/dp/1638718458

As one pre-publication reader noted: "I was hooked to the story upon reading the first chapter. I really wanted to learn more about Grace and her daughter, Bella, following the death of Bill. It was a shock to see that the story follows John, the man who killed Bill. However, it was more of a positive reaction rather than one of disappointment. Though the point of views of the two parts are different, there is a nice flow to it … Right from the start in Chapter 1, the story pulls you in. The letter is intense and heartfelt. I could feel Grace's pain. When I started reading Chapter 2 and realized that this story is about John and his perspective of what happened, I definitely wanted to keep reading."

While Grace is the central character in the first book, John narrates this one. Grace's story was an exceptionally thought-provoking and intriguing tale of heartbreak and hope. It left readers cheering for Grace while abhorring John. For this second installment of Betty Collier's book series, she flips the script. The once repugnant antagonist, John, will tug at the reader's heartstrings. Although Grace will remain a beloved figure throughout the book series, one will walk away from Book 2 wondering how they grew to forgive and, perhaps, even love John too.

This is a captivating story of grace, love, forgiveness, and redemption. If you have struggled with any of these, you will find answers embedded within these pages.

~

Visit Betty's website at livinginsidethetestimony.com for the latest information about *The Birthday Gift* book series. You will find links on her website to connect with her on social media as well.

Each book in this series is told by a different narrator, all of whom were originally introduced in the first book. They are breakaway sequels that will capture your attention while taking you on emotional roller coasters you're not soon to forget.

Book 1 - The Birthday Gift
Book 2 - Dear John
Book 3 - I Can Only Imagine: Bella's Journey (2023)
Book 4 - Mary, Did You Know? (2024)
Book 5 - WILL Is a Gift from God (2025)

Chapter 1
The Grace Letter

Grace Williams
7983 Fairview Lane
Laguna Niguel, CA 92677

Dear John,

As much as I would like to hate you and wish that you would rot in hell, I simply cannot do that. Quite frankly, I'm ashamed to admit that I once felt that way at all. You see, I am the widow of the wonderful man you so callously killed in the bathroom at Heathrow Airport with no regard whatsoever to the precious life you took so senselessly and selfishly for no reason.

Bill was unequivocally the absolute love of my life, and I expected to grow old with him. I will be forty-two next month, and I anticipated spending my next forty-two years with him. All our hopes and dreams were shattered on that abysmal day when you decided to commit what I previously thought was an unforgiveable sin.

Several months have passed since that day, and I have a new outlook on life now. Of course I am aware of what's been happening in London. From what the

Grace Williams
7983 Fairview Lane
Laguna Niguel, CA 92677

police have told me, I expect that you will live the rest of your days behind bars. Your freedom has been stripped away as it should have been. You deserve nothing but the harshest of punishments and the longest sentence allowed by law.

I have no say on the matter and trust the criminal justice system will work to prevent you from destroying anyone else's life. You destroyed my life by taking Bill away from me. His sixteen-year-old daughter still cries herself to sleep some nights. Our world came crashing down on us because of your evil act, and I almost lost my will to live.

However, I know that I cannot live the victorious life that God has planned for me with this hatred and bitterness in my heart toward you. In order for me to move on with my life, I need to be able to forgive you. Quite frankly, I never wanted to forgive you, but I know I must for my own peace of mind.

For by grace are ye saved through faith; and that not of yourselves: it is the gift of God.
Ephesians 2:8

Grace Williams
7983 Fairview Lane
Laguna Niguel, CA 92677

The police told me that you were extremely remorseful about what you did. Your remorse is no consolation for me though because it doesn't bring my husband back. You should have thought about that before you ruthlessly used his own cane to smack him in the head so merciless like that. If you wanted his laptop, why didn't you just snatch it and run? You knew very well that he was not able to chase after you because he walked with a cane.

I've gone to counseling at my church, and I've asked God to forgive me for having unhealthy acrimonious feelings toward you. I wanted you to suffer with every breath you take, and I wanted all your days and nights to be filled with tormenting pictures of Bill's lifeless body lying there on the restroom floor. It would have made me deliriously happy to hear that you took your own life or that some other prisoner did to you what you did to Bill.

I must say it was at that point that I really began to

Grace Williams
7983 Fairview Lane
Laguna Niguel, CA 92677

seek the Lord for guidance and forgiveness because I believe that life is precious and should be valued above anything else. While I will never understand why you committed such a malevolent act, I have accepted the fact that I can only be responsible for how I respond to your actions.

It is only because of God's love, his grace, and his mercy that I can say with all sincerity that I forgive you, John. I pray that you will be able to find a sense of peace and forgive yourself. If you have not asked God to forgive you, I wholeheartedly encourage you to do so. No sin is too great or so abominable that God will not forgive.

As a matter of fact, God wants to forgive you. All you have to do is ask. Then you can have peace right here on earth and eternal life with him in heaven. I discovered over these past few months of grieving my insuperable loss that I did not have peace in my mind. By forgiving you and sending this letter, I am now free.

For by grace are ye saved through faith; and that not of yourselves: it is the gift of God.
Ephesians 2:8

Grace Williams
7983 Fairview Lane
Laguna Niguel, CA 92677

I can move forward with a renewed spirit and joy in my life again.

Speaking of joy, I have enclosed a copy of what you were looking for in Bill's laptop. I know you overheard him on the phone at the airport when he left me that voice mail about finding a priceless, life-changing birthday gift for our daughter, Bella. It wasn't hidden "inside" his laptop though, so no matter how hard you looked, you never would have found it. The gift was actually a sculpture of the Gospel Symbol. You will see a picture of it and an explanation of what it means in the additional information I included with this letter.

Please look carefully! The Gospel Symbol is breathtaking. It is certainly priceless. I pray that it will change your life. What you were looking for never existed; however, this is actually all that you will ever need. John, you need Christ in your life! This symbol shows you exactly how to accomplish that. I pray that you read every word so that you fully understand what this means to

For by grace are ye saved through faith; and that not of yourselves: it is the gift of God.
Ephesians 2:8

Grace Williams
7983 Fairview Lane
Laguna Niguel, CA 92677

you on a personal level.

It's not too late for you to have a covenant relationship with Jesus. I pray that you accept Jesus Christ as your Lord and Savior this day, whatever day it is that you are reading this letter. You took Bill's life because you thought he had a priceless gift hidden inside his laptop. I pray that you discover the priceless gift of everlasting life. Bill's death should not be in vain. Jesus dying on the cross to save you from your sin should not be in vain either.

I doubt if I ever reach out to you again. I have said all I need to say. I forgive you and pray that you find the love of God in your heart. I trust that the Lord's will be done in your life as I move forward with mine. I have to put this behind me and focus on my future without Bill. My daughter and I will carry on without him but certainly in memory of him. We will spread the Gospel around the world as a testimony of God's great love for ALL of humanity.

For by grace are ye saved through faith; and that not of yourselves: it is the gift of God.
Ephesians 2:8

Grace Williams
7983 Fairview Lane
Laguna Niguel, CA 92677

As I close, I just want you to know that Bill's death is not the end of his story. He is in heaven looking down on us. I can feel his undying love and his comforting presence all around me and inside me. I know he never would have chosen to leave Bella and me so suddenly and so soon.

Sometimes we may not always understand why God allows certain things to happen, but we can always trust that it is for a reason. Therefore, it gives me great pleasure to inform you of the joyous news I was not able to share with my husband. My dearly beloved son, the miracle child Bill and I never thought we could conceive after his accident in the Navy, is due to make his arrival any day now. Bill's legacy will live on through our precious baby boy, William Matthew Williams III.

Very sincerely,

Grace

For by grace are ye saved through faith; and that not of yourselves: it is the gift of God.
Ephesians 2:8

Chapter 2

What an (Un)forgettable Day!

I wept.

I wailed.

I wept and wailed.

What Mrs. Williams didn't understand is that I did not intentionally kill her husband that disastrous day when our paths never should have crossed. On the contrary, I am quite possibly one of the most unlikely people on earth to knowingly commit such a heinous atrocity.

After reading that unexpected letter from Grace, I immediately thought about the single most horrendous day of my life. I've not yet been able to fully comprehend what possessed me to perpetrate such a reprehensible act. I don't know what I was thinking when I followed Bill into the bathroom at the airport. All I wanted was to catch a glimpse of the priceless, life-changing gift I overheard him telling his wife about on the phone.

What came over me? Why did I reach for his laptop case? How could my curiosity lead to an innocent man's death?

I sat there on the cot in my prison cell engulfed in a pool of tears. My weeping and wailing exacerbated for several minutes. I lamented over that letter, which traveled all the way from California to reach me in London. It was supposed to be quiet time, yet I was getting louder and louder with my uncontrollable wailing.

Eventually, frantic footsteps pounded down the hall, barreling toward me. Two guards bolted through my door, yelling profanities because I had broken the silence rules. Out of frustration, they threw me head first against the concrete wall. With blood streaming down my face, I briefly made eye contact with one of them before he clobbered me in the nose. My listless body crashed to the floor.

I woke up in solitary confinement and found myself bound in a straitjacket.

After awakening, the last several months of my life flashed through my mind like I was watching a Lifetime movie. Alone in the hole, I replayed those ghastly details. I began talking as if I was telling someone else how I wound up in prison. Many of the details are vivid, but to this day, I am still a bit confused about how some of the specifics unfolded.

I could hear myself telling my side of the story, albeit vastly different from Grace's perspective, but no one was there to listen.

It all began one Wednesday morning at the airport after I overheard part of a voicemail another passenger left for his wife. As we were waiting to board a flight from London to Los Angeles, he told her that he had found a priceless, life-changing gift for their daughter's birthday at a flea market in Tel Aviv. He didn't say what it was, though. He said he had hidden it in his laptop so she wouldn't discover it when he arrived home. I was curious as to what that priceless gift could have been, so I followed him to the bathroom.

Once inside the bathroom, I lunged for the case. Bill jumped as he turned to look at me, and somehow, I snatched his cane instead of the case, which was in his other hand. As I was pulling with all my might, I slipped. The cane flew out of my grip, striking him in the center of his forehead. His limp body crumpled to the floor. With my heart pounding, I grabbed his laptop that had fallen out the case and shoved it into my own laptop case. With one quick backward glance, I took off, leaving him passed out right there in the bathroom.

Discombobulated, all I could think of was that I had to get out of London and back home to Tel Aviv. So that's what I did. I fled the airport in a taxi and went back to the same hotel I had checked out of earlier that morning. Somehow, I managed to go online and purchase an airline ticket before I fell into a deep but haunted sleep. The next morning, I returned to Heathrow Airport, boarded a flight to Tel Aviv, and was back home by Thursday evening.

As I walked in the door, I was shaking, my usually neat hair a mess.

Elizabeth stared at me in disbelief. "I thought you were supposed to be in Los Angeles? What happened?"

I shrugged, trying to ignore her. How would I ever explain my return home four days early? Thoughts tumbled through my mind like clothes in a dryer.

My trip to LA had actually started two days prior, on Tuesday. Because there was a connecting flight from Tel Aviv to LA by way of London, I had worked into my itinerary an overnight stay in London. When I called my wife Tuesday night, I detailed the delightful hop-on, hop-off bus tour I had thoroughly enjoyed. It was the perfect way to see the city's most popular tourist attractions all in one day. She squealed with excitement as I described the sights, sounds, and smells at Buckingham Palace. The pictures I emailed her certainly didn't capture those details.

We had even discussed planning a trip back to England for vacation the following year. With any luck, perhaps we could go when King Charles was making a public appearance. We sorely regretted never vacationing in the United Kingdom during Queen Elizabeth's reign.

At any rate, since my journey started off so well, my dear Elizabeth wasn't concerned at first; however, when she didn't hear from me Wednesday, letting her know I had arrived safely in the United States, she became concerned. Her concern turned to worry and eventually to fear. After calling me no less than two dozen times with no response, she panicked.

In preparation for boarding the flight at Heathrow to LA, I turned my phone off. I followed Bill to the bathroom a few minutes after that. I never turned my phone back on until I returned home in Tel Aviv. No wonder she was a ball of nerves after her calls all went straight to voicemail.

So even though it was a mere two days since I'd originally left home, it felt as if I had not slept in a week. Elizabeth was crying. I suspect she had been crying most of the day because she didn't know what was happening or if I was safe. When she called the hotel in LA to find out if I had checked in, they would not give her any information. The airline wouldn't confirm if I had boarded the flight, either.

We collapsed in each other's arms and sat on the sofa for what seemed like hours.

That's all I recalled initially when I returned so unexpectedly to Israel. I was home with my beloved Elizabeth, and whatever happened could be sorted out later. All I wanted to do was rest in her warm embrace and get some much-needed sleep. The last thing I remembered hearing her say before I drifted off that night was that she knew she should have traveled to Los Angeles with me.

Friday morning arrived much too soon. I woke up hungry and confused. I turned to my beautiful Elizabeth right by my side, as always. She was still asleep. I had forgotten what transpired at the airport and was still confused about being back in Tel Aviv. I vaguely remembered taking the train to the airport on Monday, no Tuesday… or was it Wednesday?

Tuesday.

Yes, it was Tuesday. I left Tel Aviv on Tuesday to spend not much more than twenty-four hours in London, and then I was going to finish my trip from London to LA on Wednesday. Why I was back home in my own bed Friday morning was a disturbing mystery to me at the time.

I snuggled closer to Elizabeth and wrapped my arms around her while she slept. She could feel me in her sleep, as usual, and reciprocated by pressing her body against mine with her head nestled sweetly in my chest.

"Just breathe, John. Just breathe." I had to constantly remind myself to calm down and breathe to prevent setting off any alarms that something could be amiss.

The only truth I knew right then was that I was home, embracing my wife whom I loved beyond my vocabulary. She was flawless, just like a diamond. God had sent me an extraordinary being to walk this earth by my side. Surely, there was a logical explanation for my unexpected return home to this remarkable woman who had always loved me unconditionally, flaws and all.

Chapter 3

Home Sweet Home

While Elizabeth slept, I lay there for a while and tried to remember what happened on Wednesday that caused me to fly back home the next day. Was my flight canceled? Did I sleep at the airport overnight, waiting for it to be rescheduled? Did I miss the boarding call? As hard as I tried to recall those missing links, there was nothing but a black hole in my memory. For some unbeknownst reason, I had come back home instead of continuing with my plans to go to Los Angeles to meet with the Board of Rabbis of Southern California.

I was in the shower when Elizabeth woke up. I heard her call out for me, but her voice was quivering like someone who had seen a ghost. Not wanting to cause her any additional distress, I decided not to tell her I had no idea why I had come back home. I simply responded that I would be out of the shower in a few minutes. I didn't recall if I had even taken a shower the day before. Honestly, I think I had arrived home in the same clothes I wore to the airport on Wednesday.

After getting dressed, I followed the aroma to the kitchen where I found Elizabeth making shakshuka for breakfast. It was my favorite. She had bags under her eyes. I wondered how much sleep she had gotten the night before. I offered to help with breakfast, but she declined.

Then she asked, "My dear John, why didn't you go to Los Angeles as planned?"

I blurted out the first thing that came to mind: "The meeting got canceled at the last minute. When I landed in LA, I had a voicemail waiting for me from Rabbi Bernstein. He said he hoped he wasn't too late notifying me that Rabbi Shapira had taken gravely ill. The meeting would need to be rescheduled."

I felt terrible for not telling her the truth, but at the time, I didn't know what the truth was. I had caused enough anguish already and didn't want her to worry needlessly.

I devoured my breakfast as if I had not eaten in a week. My mind started racing again, and I was exhausted. I had no idea how I was going to play this off.

What if I got a phone call from someone on the board that morning asking if I had been delayed after not showing up for the 10:00 meeting? After all, the meeting was still supposed to take place. I just didn't want Elizabeth to know. What if she overheard me talking to them? I needed to make a phone call to the board before they called me.

Even though I was extremely sluggish, I told Elizabeth I needed to go for a walk to stretch my legs because of jet lag. I said that quick turnaround trip had thrown me out of kilter. She wasn't suspicious at all. I changed my shoes and left the house with a water bottle and my cell. When I was safely around the corner, I called one of the rabbis that I was scheduled to meet. I had to leave a voicemail. I called another. It went to voicemail also. I called the main number at the office, and no one answered. Where was everyone? I needed to talk to them while I was away from Elizabeth so she would not potentially hear me talking to them later.

Then it dawned on me. It was still Thursday night in Los Angeles. Tel Aviv was ten hours ahead. I hoped they would hear my voicemails when they got up Friday morning and not call me back at an inopportune time when I would be unable to talk freely. Hopefully, the story I made up in the message would suffice.

I was feeling quite weary and certainly had no desire to go for a walk, but I did anyway. I was hoping something would jog my memory while I was out in the fresh air. Unfortunately, that didn't happen. I became more confused and frustrated with every step I took. I gave up and returned home. I told Elizabeth I was drained and needed a nap. She was in her office taking care of some business, so I retreated to our bedroom.

My heart was racing when I awakened in a cold sweat. I looked at the clock and realized I had been asleep for almost four hours. Elizabeth's note right next to the clock on the nightstand said she had gone to Tzarfati's to pick up some fresh fish for dinner. She knew how much I loved any fresh catch of the day from that place.

Tzarfati's Fish of the Sea was located in the Jaffa Flea Market.

I had just dreamed about the Jaffa Flea Market. What a coincidence.

Then it hit me like a ton of bricks.

A piece of the black hole suddenly came to light. A man's voice with an American accent echoed in my head. He told someone he found a precious, life changing gift at the Jaffa Flea Market, of all places! Elizabeth and I had been there on numerous occasions through the years. While the trinkets made nice souvenirs for tourists, I doubted there was anything of real value, surely nothing priceless or life-changing.

The conversation began to play over and over again in my mind. I couldn't get that voice out of my head. It felt like I was sitting in the airport again, and his voice was getting louder and louder as if he was sitting right next to me.

"Good morning, Mrs. Williams. You won't believe what I found for Bella's birthday."

Now tormented by that voice, I could actually see his face. He was talking on the phone to someone named Mrs. Williams. I thought it was his wife, but why would he call her Mrs. Williams instead of her first name? I think he even called her "sweetie" during that strange voicemail he had left her. It sure sounded like Bella was their daughter, and he had hidden something of tremendous value for her in his laptop.

I couldn't help but wonder what he was hiding.

Chapter 4

Who Was That?

Did I dream all of that, or was it true? Did I overhear a phone call at the airport which changed the trajectory of my travel plans? Indubitably, that had nothing to do with my returning home instead of going to LA. Who was that man?

And why did I feel sick to my stomach every time I remembered his voice?

Elizabeth walked in a few minutes later and startled me. My hands were shaking, and I was a bit short of breath. She became concerned, but I told her I had just awakened from a bad dream. I shrugged it off as insignificant and assumed it was simply my mind playing tricks on me. I told Elizabeth that I was going to unpack while she prepared dinner.

Where was my laptop? I had not checked my email for a couple of days and didn't want to sort everything out on that tiny cell phone screen. I saw my overnight bag sitting in the corner of the bedroom. I had gone through it earlier that morning looking for my toiletries. My laptop wasn't in there. I looked in my big suitcase, and there it was. I forgot I had put it in there after I landed in Tel Aviv to make it easier when I caught a ride from the airport.

Whew! It was a good thing I had not lost it. With the way the past couple of days had been going, I would not have been the least bit surprised if I had left my laptop in London. I sat the case on the dresser for later and put everything away from my other two bags. Feeling lethargic again, I lay across the bed for a few minutes and must have dozed off. I was awakened by Elizabeth calling out to say dinner was ready. My laptop case was still sitting on the dresser when I joined Elizabeth for dinner.

What a delightful evening we had. She took my mind off my confusion without even knowing it. It was getting late, and I didn't feel like checking my email anymore. We settled in and watched television for a while. I didn't get any phone calls from the rabbis that evening either, so all was well. I watched the clock, and once I knew it was well past the time they would have called me, I could breathe a sigh of relief. I had survived another day. For the time being, I hid my bewilderment from Elizabeth. This state of confusion had to be temporary. I just needed some rest.

Apparently, I needed quite a bit of rest. It was 3:00 a.m. when I lurched up from the sofa. We had both fallen asleep watching TV. Had it not been for that man's voice in my dream, I probably would have slept all night on the sofa. When I jumped up, I woke up my wife.

"Dear John, what's wrong with you?"

I told her it was another bad dream. Being married to this woman for the past twenty-one years, I should have known better than to admit to having yet another bad dream. She knew my dreams were sometimes associated with bouts of confusion and disorientation. The dreams always seemed real.

I tried to assure her it was likely due to my trip and that I would be fine once I caught up on my sleep. I held her ever so closely, and she soon fell sound asleep in my arms. I, on the other hand, didn't get another minute of sleep for the rest of the night.

I was relieved when Saturday morning finally came, but I didn't know why. Elizabeth got dressed early and left for a meeting right after breakfast. She didn't know I had spent half the night wide awake. Why trouble her? I had already done enough damage.

After she was gone, I decided to tackle my emails. I wondered what I had missed over the past few days. When I opened my case to get my laptop out, I dropped it on the floor. It was heavier than usual. I don't know why I didn't notice that the day before.

I looked down at my bedroom floor, and much to my surprise and dismay, there were two laptops there.

"Oh, God!"

Chapter 5

It Was Not a Dream

What in the world had I done?

As I collapsed to the floor beside both laptops, I heard myself screaming in my mind, but the words would not come out of my mouth: "What have I done this time?"

What had I done to end up with two laptops? Only one belonged to me. Where did the other one come from, and where was its owner? I've never stolen anything in my life. Well, not that I was aware of. This made no sense at all.

In the midst of my confusion, while wallowing around on the floor, that man's voice began to vex me. It got more intense with each passing second. He was beyond enthusiastic and spoke with such jubilee, as if he had found a hidden treasure more valuable than anything on earth.

"Good morning, Mrs. Williams. You won't believe what I found for Bella's birthday."

Then I saw it. I saw his name engraved on the mystery laptop.

Bill Williams
Faith Productions

My head pounded. My heart raced. My hands trembled My feet were numb. My breath came in short gasps. My vision was blurry. My room was black.

Then, in the midst of my distress, another part of my memory came back.

Bill Williams was the American in my dream. Unfortunately, Bill Williams was *not* a dream. He was real. He was at the airport in London waiting for the same flight to Los Angeles. Mrs. Williams was his wife, and Bella was their daughter whose birthday was coming.

I was his assailant.

Why I took his laptop, I will never know. I just know that I did, and then I dashed out of the bathroom as if nothing happened. When I heard that awful thud of his cane hitting his forehead, I panicked and ran.

No wonder his voice was haunting me. I had to figure out how to return the laptop.

I assumed he filed a report at the airport. All I had to do was contact the airport's Lost and Found department. I couldn't exactly tell them the truth, though. I was much too embarrassed. The best way to handle this awkwardness was to say that when I unpacked my bags, I discovered I had someone else's laptop. I would pretend there must have been a mix-up when we went through security and had to place our laptops on the conveyor belt. I must have mistakenly grabbed the wrong one.

No one would ever need to know the whole truth about what actually happened in the bathroom.

Perhaps they would assume Bill slipped and hit his head. After all, he did walk with a cane. I couldn't admit to being involved in another mysterious situation. They would start their assessment and probing all over. I had grown more than weary of the entire intrusive process. It had not even been three months prior that they changed my medication the last time. I absolutely could not bear putting Elizabeth through that all over again.

Thankfully, she wasn't home when I found the laptop. I would be able to take care of this unfortunate predicament very discretely. There was no need for Elizabeth to know about yet another disconcerting quandary.

I grabbed my laptop and searched for the lost property phone number at Heathrow. They would give me easy instructions for how best to return that laptop. Much to my disappointment, the website said office hours were now temporarily limited to Monday – Friday, 9:00 a.m. until 3:00 p.m. I'd have to wait two more days. It was only Saturday, although it felt like my transgression had happened a month ago.

Maybe I could find Bill's phone number myself and just call him. He should be happy I found his laptop. Since he was headed to Los Angeles, maybe that's where he lived. Faith Productions. Apparently, that's where he worked. I searched the internet, but quickly discovered I would need more information to narrow down my search. I had no idea his name and the company name were both so common in LA.

I looked at the clock in a bit of distress. Time was running out. Elizabeth would be home from her meeting soon. I started sweating. I felt a panic attack coming on. All I had to do was calm down, hide the laptop, and just wait until Monday. For whatever reason, I found myself unable to do that. With each passing second, it felt as if the room was caving in on me.

That's when I saw a vision of Bill. He had not fainted as I previously thought.

He was *dead.*

"Oh God, no! Please, noo!"

I tossed the laptop against the wall, then scurried over to pick it up and hurled it against the wall on the other side of the room. I was trying to make his voice stop so I would stop seeing his deceased body. It seemed like a hallucination. I was determined not to lose complete control. There was no way he could be dead. He had simply passed out from the blow to the head. Never would I have walked out of the bathroom without trying to help him if I'd thought it had been more serious.

"Good morning, Mrs. Williams. You won't believe what I found for Bella's birthday."

"Good morning, Mrs. Williams. You won't believe what I found for Bella's birthday."

"Good morning, Mrs. Williams. You won't believe what I found for Bella's birthday."

He wouldn't stop saying that. I started beating the laptop with whatever I could grab. Using my own laptop like a hammer, I thought I could smash it enough to erase the memory or stop the hallucinations. I broke a lamp in the process. The dresser mirror shattered as it crashed to the floor. I don't even know if I was breathing at that point. I looked down at my hands. Blood gushed out of my wrist. Someone or something had overpowered me. I had lost all control and was as helpless as a newborn baby. I somberly surrendered. There was no fight left in me.

I had literally destroyed my own bedroom. Both laptops were all but unrecognizable. I didn't know where I'd cut my head, or how, but blood streamed down my face, and my hands were covered with it. The room was silent. I knew for certain that Bill had perished.

I had his blood on my hands.

Chapter 6

Dear God

"Oh, *dear God… John!"*

It was Elizabeth.

She had to step over broken glass to reach me. I was trembling in the corner of the bedroom. I didn't know how long I had been there. Unaware of time or space at that moment, I thought I had experienced an out of body phenomenon. My life was over. I was going to hell.

While sobbing uncontrollably, Elizabeth was also tying a tourniquet to stop the bleeding and tending to my other wounds.

I must have lost a great deal of blood, because I woke up at Ichilov Hospital. The first thing I saw was a nurse connecting a pint of blood to my IV. I screamed loudly in my head, "What happened?" but no one heard me. Maybe I had only screamed in my head. I couldn't tell. The nurse continued what she was doing, and then I heard her say, "Mrs. Batista, this is the last pint of blood before they do the other tests."

Mrs. Batista? That was my angel, Elizabeth. Where was she? I tried sitting up in bed to find her, but I couldn't raise my head. I tried reaching for her, but my hands wouldn't move. I tried calling out her name, but no sound came out of my mouth.

Panic spiraled through me. *What is wrong with me?*

As soon as the nurse left, Elizabeth appeared within my field of vision. She must have been sitting by the window while the nurse gave me the blood. She grabbed my hand at once. Her eyes were red and swollen, her makeup smeared. Her eyes were still glassy. I tried to tell her how sorry I was and that I loved her more than life itself and wished I could have spared her all of this trauma. Yet still, no words came out of my mouth. My lips did not even move.

Was I paralyzed?

Was I in a coma?

Or was I being punished for committing the unforgiveable?

It was all clear now. I knew what I had done, but I was unable to tell anyone. My voice was gone, but I could hear hers. She prayed as she caressed my hand. All I could do was look at her. She was my entire world. When God gave her to me, he knew she was all I needed. She loved me unconditionally.

As her tears dropped onto my hand, I spontaneously squeezed hers. Our eyes locked. We both knew everything was going to be all right. Overwhelming peace swept over both of us as we began crying. In my mind, I assured her that I had come to terms with what happened. I would face the consequences for killing Bill, but ultimately my fate was in God's hands. However, she couldn't read my thoughts, but it sure felt like she touched my soul. As I drifted back to sleep, I was at peace.

Moments later, Elizabeth's voice woke me. I only caught a few words, but "prognosis" stood out as did her tearful remarks that I hadn't uttered a single word for the entire week I'd been there.

The doctor had no answers. He simply said we'd all have to wait and see.

I had a dream that night.

I was in Los Angeles meeting with the Board of Rabbis. Due to a budget crisis several years prior, they had been able to amend state regulations so that non-ordained rabbis could serve as chaplains. I was an ideal candidate and highly qualified to provide guidance to prisoners based on my work experience in Tel Aviv. They were very interested in having Elizabeth and me move to LA so that I could serve in this new role for the California Department of Corrections.

Rabbi Bernstein said there was a severe shortage of Jewish chaplains, and the spiritual needs of many Jewish prisoners were not being met. Serving in an institutionalized setting had inherent challenges, of course. There was a rising Jewish prison population, especially in the federal system, but California budget cuts had eliminated most of the vacant chaplain positions.

It had been over twenty years since I'd lived in California. What would returning home to the USA be like? There would certainly be some culture shock, but this was the perfect opportunity. They desperately needed a visible Jewish presence to protect the vulnerable inmates who were often subjected to neo-Nazi gangs and white supremacists.

The inmates were already suffering many atrocities, and I wanted to provide them with the guidance and education they needed while incarcerated. God knew their spiritual needs were not being met. I wanted them to be able to leave better than when they entered the system. Trying to reenter society was hard enough. One of the last things they'd need was to feel abandoned by the Jewish community.

My dream seemed to last for days, much longer than my planned meeting with the Board. I think I was in an alternate state of partial dreaming and partial fantasizing about what my meeting would have been like had I made that trip to Los Angeles. The best part of the dream was when they offered me the position. The worst part was when my dream turned into a nightmare.

I became one of those forsaken Jewish prisoners.

Chapter 7

The Beginning of the End

I woke up thrashing about and screaming for my life.

With all the commotion, I'm surprised Elizabeth didn't bolt out of the room. She'd been fast asleep in that tiny hospital bed with me. As soon as my cries for help woke her, she began to console me as she stroked my face ever so gently. I don't know who was trembling more, but it felt as if we were doing it in unison. Our connection with each other was undeniable. I soon caught my breath, and for a brief moment, all felt right with the world.

After Elizabeth left the room to talk to the nurse, I had a few minutes to collect my thoughts. It seemed all of my afflictions were gone. As trapped as I had felt in my body before I had that dream, I now felt completely free. I was able to talk again. I was able to move again.

Sadly, I was also able to remember everything.

I had not left Bill Williams passed out on the bathroom floor. I left him dead.

My mind was playing exceptionally dangerous and deadly tricks on me. The situation was dire, and the best thing to do would be to get out of that hospital. I needed time alone with Elizabeth to explain what happened and figure out what to do next.

I tried my best to remain calm when Elizabeth came bouncing back in the room with the nurse. She was eager to show her that I had awakened from whatever troubled state I had been in. The nurse performed her assessment and left the room to call my doctor. Elizabeth sat on the side of the bed with me. She looked so angelic. A bit worn and frazzled, but angelic nonetheless.

The enormous smile on her face brought tears to my eyes. I played it off and told her that I was overcome with emotions due to what had transpired from my last day at home until that day in the hospital. At the time, I had absolutely no idea I had been there for eight days.

After running a gamut of tests and adjusting my medication, they finally told me that I could go home. Ten days had passed from the day Elizabeth walked into our home and found me almost bleeding to death on our bedroom floor. I had destroyed that room trying to destroy Bill's laptop and all the memories associated with it. What was it going to be like returning home and telling Elizabeth the truth?

I was certain that my nightmare was just beginning.

As we waited for the nurse to come in with my discharge paperwork, Elizabeth gleefully sang *Hava Nagila:*

> *Let's rejoice*
> *Let's rejoice*
> *Let's rejoice and be glad*

I tried to smile, but my insides clenched, refusing to settle. How was I going to tell her what happened at the airport? I had taken an innocent man's life. My life was over, and hers was about to implode.

When we got home at lunchtime, I was shocked to see the bedroom in perfect condition. Elizabeth had taken care of everything. She wanted no bad memories to hit me in the face upon my return home. Little did she know I was living with all of those bleak memories in my head, plus many more which were quite terrifying.

I asked Elizabeth if she felt like going to the Jaffa Flea Market. She thought it was a very strange question considering all that I had endured over the past ten days. I told her I just wanted to walk around in the fresh air and take in all the sights and sounds to help clear my head from the hospital ordeal. She didn't know that was my pathetic excuse to hide my real motive.

I had met Elizabeth at that very flea market over twenty years prior. I had been an international student from the United States enrolled at Tel Aviv University as part of a year-long study abroad program. I remembered that day like it was yesterday. The university had arranged for several groups of international students to go on private tours of the flea market. I had been assigned to the group that had Elizabeth as our tour guide. When the tour was over, I stuck around, hoping to be able to initiate some kind of conversation with her.

Fortunately, our group had been her last tour of the day. When I approached her afterward, she wasn't startled. She had noticed my enthusiasm during the tour and assumed I had more questions about what we had seen. My decision to engage in a one-on-one conversation has proven to be the best decision of my life. She captured my heart that day and never let go.

Often, I found myself back at the flea market shadowing her tours because I had to be near her. Over the next few days, she began to trust me enough to spend time with me away from work.

Never in a million years had I expected her to fall in love with an American college student like me, but miraculously, she did. I wanted to relive that moment when we first met on the tour. I wanted to relive that instant when my life changed. After growing up in six different foster homes, I had no real family. Even at that age, Elizabeth instantly seemed like the family I had always yearned to have.

I completed my final year of college in Tel Aviv, and we said our temporary goodbyes. I promised Elizabeth I would return before the end of the year. Being an exceptionally gifted student in foster care came with many advantages. I had been awarded several scholarships to attend the University of California, which opened numerous doors for me. It had been easy to get the help I needed after graduation to work out the logistics of moving to Israel. They even connected me with several job opportunities there.

Surprisingly, everything worked out, and I returned to Tel Aviv, where my new life began. I left behind all the pain and anguish that had been part of my childhood. I had no one in America anyway. I converted to Judaism and, eighteen months after I first laid eyes on her at the flea market, I married my first love, my one and only love.

As I reminisced about our first encounter, Elizabeth brought me back to reality when she said an impromptu trip to the flea market would hopefully be therapeutic for me. She had no reason to doubt that I was trying to clear my head after my untoward hospitalization. The moment we met had flashed right before my eyes, and I was searching for that feeling one last time.

The afternoon sun was welcoming. We ate lunch at one of the outdoor cafes. I had reached the end of my happily-ever-after. Once we got back home, the nightmare would come back with a vengeance.

For those couple of hours, however, my life was total bliss.

Elizabeth was tired when we got home. I had not considered what that hospital ordeal had been like for her. She was such a strong little woman, much stronger than I. She asked if I would be okay while she took a quick nap. I said of course even though in the back of my mind, I was anything but okay. I told her I was feeling drained as well and asked if I could join her for a nap.

She fell asleep almost instantly. I lay there with her head buried in my chest and caressed her ever so gently. What if this was the last time she'd let me touch her? I was a murderer, albeit not intentionally, but nevertheless that's what I was. I closed my eyes and didn't want that moment to end. She was lying in what she used to tell me was her very favorite spot in the whole world, the one where she could feel my heartbeat.

My time was running out. I opened my eyes so I could watch her breathe. I closed my eyes so I could picture us growing old together. I opened my eyes so I could watch her dark, silky hair glistening in the sunlight peeping through the window. I closed my eyes and replayed our wedding day in my mind. I opened my eyes and stared at the woman God gave me. I closed my eyes as tears streamed down my face.

Elizabeth inhaled deeply, and I squeezed her tighter, as if silently begging her not to move, not to look at me. She surely felt my increasing sobs as I shuddered trying to stay in control.

"Please tell me what's going on."

I whispered, "I'm on my way to hell."

Chapter 8

Truth or Consequences

As tears continued to flow, I told her everything that happened at the airport.

She never lifted her head from my chest. Then she stroked my face and said, "Nothing has changed, John. You are, and always will be, the absolute love of my life! We will get through this together and come out even stronger on the other side."

I was expecting a much different reaction from her, something more emotional—shock, hysteria, disgust, fear, hate, disappointment, frustration, or even sheer horror that she was lying beside a murderer, whether that murder had been accidental or not.

We had to prepare for my reckoning. We knew the best course of action would be to return to Heathrow Airport for me to turn myself in to the authorities. Since I had been discharged from the hospital that day, Elizabeth felt we needed to leave for London immediately so it would not appear that I was on the run. My memory had failed me at first, and then a medical emergency ensued afterward. I needed to return to London pronto and pay the price for what I had unwittingly done.

Elizabeth said she knew she should have gone to Los Angeles with me to meet with the Board of Rabbis. We could have toured those federal prisons together over the weekend. I can't believe she felt guilty for what happened. She blamed herself for not being there with me and for me. She thought if she had been there, none of this would have happened. I knew deep in my heart that was not the case. I had made peace with what happened and blamed no one except myself.

Needless to say, she was not going to let me return to London alone. We bought our tickets and spent our final night together in Tel Aviv.

It would be the last night I ever slept on Israeli soil.

I don't know if I slept at all. My life didn't flash before my eyes, but glimpses of my childhood, going from one foster home to the next, began to replay in my mind. Emotions I assumed were locked away forever became overwhelming.

I tossed and turned for what seemed like several days, but it was still dark outside. Elizabeth slept like a baby. I was relieved that I had told her everything. Sure, it seemed implausible, but that was my reality. She didn't run away frightened, and instead, snuggled even closer and loved on me. Between the nightmares, the memories, the flashbacks, and watching her sleep, my last night at home was a roller coaster.

I was glad when daylight broke, though I knew what came next would break me.

55

Chapter 9

Fight or Flight

Our flight was perfectly normal on that beautiful, crystal-clear morning. I stared out the window, not knowing that I would never see that sacred ground again. I didn't know what to expect once we arrived in London. I guess I never thought that far ahead. All I knew was that I could no longer run from the truth.

It was a five-hour nonstop flight on Virgin Atlantic. Because of the time zone difference, we left home at 6:40 a.m. and arrived at Heathrow at 9:40 a.m. local time. Not once did Elizabeth ask any questions about what happened. We hardly talked about what we were going to do after we landed except that we would ask for the authorities to report an *incident* that happened in the bathroom two weeks prior.

Most of our conversation was reminiscing about the past, how we had first met, our wedding day, and the wonderful lives that we had built for ourselves in Tel Aviv. I barely thought about the difficult life I had once endured in America because it was too painful. College had been my saving grace. Otherwise, I don't know how I would have turned out. I never would have met Elizabeth. She was the one person in the world who loved me through my scars and flaws.

After she drifted off to sleep with her head on my shoulder, I wondered what would have happened had I made it to LA and met with the Board of Rabbis. I really wanted that position as a prison chaplain serving the Jewish inmates. It seemed to be the fresh start we needed, and the answer to our prayers.

Elizabeth had lost both of her parents in a horrible train wreck two years prior. She was their only child, and part of her died that day when she received the devastating news. Perhaps it would have been easier for her to accept their deaths had it been a simple accident. Knowing the conductor was under the influence and allowed to operate the train while impaired made it almost impossible to comprehend, let alone accept.

From the moment she received the settlement from the transit company last year, she purposed in her heart that she would leave Tel Aviv and start over somewhere else. Staying there was too painful. With money no longer an issue, all we needed to do was work out the logistics of selling her parents' lucrative tour guide business. It had been in the family for years and flourished tremendously over the last couple of decades when tourism in Tel Aviv had skyrocketed.

I could still see that eighteen-year-old girl I fell in love with on my tour of the Jaffa Flea Market. However, life had never been the same after her parents died. Her heart wasn't in the family business anymore.

California was the most logical place for us to start over.

That's part of why the job was so attractive to me. I needed something meaningful to do. I knew what feeling forsaken and all alone in this world was like. I had the compassion and training needed to make a difference in the Jewish inmates' lives. Neither of us *needed* to work anymore, but I felt the urge to give back to the Jewish community that had been so kind to embrace me.

Our plans were coming along very well, until I ruined it. While I should have been meeting with the Board of Rabbis, Elizabeth was taking care of business at home. As a matter of fact, that meeting she had on the Saturday after I first returned home was with the buyers of her parents' business. Some investors had flown in for the weekend to personally go on all the tours the company offered. I never asked her how the meeting went. Much to my dismay, I had unraveled by the time she came home from that meeting.

I looked at her and caressed her beautiful face. How could I allow her to get caught up in this horrific debacle? As I drifted off to an unsafe place, Elizabeth began to squirm. She awakened abruptly and appeared disoriented. Then she realized we were still on the plane headed to London.

With her voice quivering, she looked into my eyes and began mumbling almost incoherently. "You know I love you with all of my being and cannot imagine my life without you. I just had this frightening dream that we are making a horrible mistake showing up at the airport without calling the police first. In my dream, they yanked you off the plane, and I never saw you again!"

Her words almost took my breath away. For her sake, I remained calm and assured her that everything would be all right. I was ready to face my punishment, but neither of us had considered what that would be. I held her as close as I could, given the constraints of being on an airplane. As I wiped away her tears, I had to wipe mine also.

We were able to regain our composure before any passengers noticed what was happening. The two men sitting directly across from us on the other side of the aisle appeared to be fast asleep. As I looked around the cabin, most people were either engrossed in a movie, had their ear pods on entertaining themselves for the five-hour flight, or they were asleep. The excruciating pain Elizabeth and I were engulfed in went unnoticed.

For about the last hour of our flight, we chatted. Elizabeth said her meeting had gone very well. Plans were moving forward with the attorneys. Her parents' tour guide company was off the market. She secured a generous offer and was free to follow me into the unknown.

Little did we know, the unknown was about to come crashing down on us in the most God-awful way.

Chapter 10

Nightmare Landing

Afraid of what we would face upon disembarking the plane, we gathered our personal carry-on items and waited our turn. I gave Elizabeth a subtle wink and told her not to worry. Everything was going to work out somehow.

With a forced smile on her face, she said softly, "My dear John, I will love you no matter what, until the end of time."

Just as the first-class passengers had exited the plane, a flight attendant made an announcement. She asked the rest of us to take our seats. Apparently, there had been some commotion as they were leaving, and it was going to take a few minutes to clear up the situation.

After waiting less than a minute, my heart started pounding. I felt my legs going numb. I couldn't breathe and began gasping for air. I knew my body was going to shut down, and I was helpless to stop it. A full-blown panic attack consumed every ounce of my being the moment I saw four police officers enter the cabin.

One of them shouted as they came toward me. "John Batista! You're under arrest for the murder of William Williams!"

Elizabeth's excruciating scream split the air. "John, *no*! Please, God, *no*…"

Then everything went black.

I didn't pass out, but an overwhelming sense of inconceivable fear had my heart racing and throat closing up on me. I didn't know if I was paralyzed or too afraid to take another step. Was I losing my mind? Were they smothering me? Was this how my life would end?

Little did I know, as two of the police officers dragged me off the plane in my rapidly deteriorating state, the other two approached Elizabeth and took her into custody. I would learn later that they didn't technically arrest her, but they brought her in for questioning.

My nightmare began the moment they called my name and escalated with each passing second. I didn't notice I was handcuffed until I was inside the police car. My trembling hands proved useless. I don't think I would have been able to use them even if they had been free. The officers must have assumed I was putting on a show; however, I continued to decline. I heard the officers laughing. One said I was acting like a fish out of water.

"Just look at him! Does he really think we're going to fall for that? I've seen better acting coming from my four-year-old trying to explain how our dog ate all the Oreos."

Perhaps an hour later, I awakened, only to hear someone say that I'd had a grand mal seizure in the back of the police car. My head was throbbing, and as I reached up to rub my forehead, I realized my hands and feet were shackled to the bed. I closed my eyes, as there wasn't a reason to open them. My life was over. I might as well have been dead. At that disastrous moment, I wished that to be true.

As soon as they proved I was medically stable, they transported me for processing in that British prison. I don't know what medication had been pumped into my body, but I was calm. Breathing was simple and effortless. I was shackled, but at least I could move my fingers and toes. The paralyzing thoughts that had overwhelmed me on the plane seemed to be a distant memory.

Apparently, when I had the seizure in police custody, they didn't try to help me at all. I felt a long row of tight sutures pulling in my forehead above my left eyebrow. I assumed I must have banged my head against the glass or bars or whatever separated me from the front seat. I told myself it could have been much worse. I could have died. Then I found myself thankful to be alive. There must have been a reason I survived that harrowing ordeal, even though it was unfathomable at the time what that reason was going to be.

Chapter 11

Answer My Question!

Once I arrived at the police station, I sat in silence, trying to comprehend what happened. I was alone in a cell under continuous observation due to the seizure. It had to be at least twenty-four hours later when the weight of what I faced slammed into me.

They took me to a different room for questioning. I'll never forget those words:

> *"You do not have to say anything. But it may harm your defense if you do not mention when questioned something, which you later rely on in court. Anything you do say may be given in evidence."*

It didn't matter what they said, though. I was having difficulty comprehending the whole situation. I don't know how I ever thought I could return to London after being gone two weeks, confess about the incident, and not be charged with murder. From the looks of things, they planned to throw the book at me and lock me up for the rest of my life.

That had not been what Elizabeth and I expected when we left Tel Aviv.

My heart stopped.

Elizabeth!

Where was she? What happened to her?

Those cries had been the last time I heard her voice. Her screams echoed in my head. How long ago had that been? My concept of time was lost. They told me I didn't have to say anything, but they were asking me questions. The only words I could muster up was, "Where is my wife?"

"We're the ones asking you questions, Batista! Don't try my patience with you! Don't you dare try my patience!"

I looked at that enraged officer with his fists clenched and veins bulging out of his neck. He slammed both hands down on the table and looked like a raging bull.

With my voice trembling, I stated as calmly as I could that I would be happy to answer all his questions. I simply needed to know what happened to my wife. He ignored my question and proceeded with his *speech* outlining my rights.

I listened, but with increasing confusion and frustration, I resorted to requesting legal counsel. They wouldn't tell me where Elizabeth was, and I had no idea how the criminal justice system worked in London. I thought it was best to keep my mouth shut and ask for an attorney.

That red-faced, infuriated officer took his paperwork and stormed out the room, slamming the door. I sat there in complete silence, not knowing what to expect. I knew what I had done and hated myself for doing it. I wanted nothing more than for that day never to have happened. Yes, I had taken an innocent man's life, but they should at least tell me where Elizabeth was.

Then I realized I had no rights. I was a murderer to them, and they must have thought I had been on the run for two weeks. No wonder they had no patience with me. No wonder they thought I was faking not being able to breathe. No wonder that officer left the room displaying his utter disgust toward me. In his eyes, I was a disgusting man who had committed the most unforgiveable sin.

That damnable thought dumbfounded me.

My life was truly over.

I was going to rot in jail and then rot in hell.

I sank ever so low in my seat and buried my head in my arms on the table.

A different officer came in a few minutes later and escorted me back to my cell. About an hour after that, someone showed up and inquired about my request for legal counsel. He explained that in England, solicitors are one of the two types of practicing lawyers. The other was called a barrister, one who pleads cases before the court. I didn't know what to do, so I accepted their offer to obtain a solicitor from the Defense Solicitor Call Center (DSCC). That would start the process, but more importantly, the solicitor should be able to locate Elizabeth for me.

Within a couple of hours, the solicitor from the DSCC arrived. He introduced himself as Mr. Hart. He was my only hope, so I had to trust him. Although he had many questions for me, my one and only question for him was if he could find out what happened to Elizabeth. He assured me he would. Then we began to talk about my case, and I told him everything.

As I spoke, I had to admit it sounded like a work of fiction. Would he think I was a deranged, cold-blooded killer? A psychopath? A nincompoop? No one could make up a cockamamie story like that. It was my real life, though, and now my consequences to suffer. I had no idea how bad it was until I heard myself tell Mr. Hart the outrageous sequence of events. For the time being, I just needed to know Elizabeth was okay, while I faced the reality that I might never be okay again.

Chapter 12

Please Don't Take My Sunshine Away

Two days later, Mr. Hart returned, accompanied by the brightest ray of sunshine I had ever seen in my entire life. He had not only kept his word but he brought Elizabeth with him. Although we were separated by a glass barrier, I could feel her just by looking into her gorgeous brown eyes and began singing.

You are my sunshine, my only sunshine.
You make me happy when skies are gray.
You'll never know, dear, how much I love you….

It was the next line of the song that almost killed me.

Please don't take my sunshine away.

They could do whatever they wanted with me, as long as I knew my wife was safe and her freedom secured.

Elizabeth reassured me with words I did not deserve. "Don't worry, my love. I will be with you until the end of time, even if the sun doesn't shine."

As I sat there, gazing through her eyes so deeply that she touched my soul, Mr. Hart interrupted my euphoric state.

"We have a great deal to discuss, but we only have thirty minutes left. Let's get down to business."

The only business I cared about pertained to my wife. She tried to convince me she was fine. They had questioned her after taking her off the plane and said she was free to go. However, they told her not to leave London until further notice but gave no timeframe as to how long that might be. She assured me she had no plans to leave, not as long as I was there. She had already checked into a hotel, and now that she knew which prison I was being housed at, she planned to find something closer.

Regardless of what happened, I had peace knowing they had no plans to charge Elizabeth with a crime. Mr. Hart explained the next steps in their criminal justice system. My first hearing would be at a Magistrate's court. He was almost certain bail would be refused by the court. Then I would be remanded in custody until my actual court hearing. Much to my dismay, that meant I would likely remain in prison until the trial or sentencing hearing took place.

Mr. Hart thought he could get the charge lowered from murder to manslaughter. Even though it appeared I had been on the run for two weeks, the police had since learned it was an accident. I had no memory of it at first, and then I had a medical emergency in Tel Aviv delaying my return to confess. Murder charges would not hold up in court.

He said since I was not aware that my actions had caused Bill's death, he could argue automatism as my defense.

That was rarely used in proceedings similar to mine, but it should work. Automatism could apply if a defendant was not aware of his actions when committing the offense.

If I was found guilty—and I would be, since I admitted to what I had done—they would impose one of two types of sentences. For indictable offenses brought to a jury, a guilty plea had to be made within twenty-eight days after the prosecutor stated compliance with Section 3 of CPIA 1996 and serving disclosure. We were well within that timeframe.

Elizabeth began rubbing the nape of her neck, unable to sit still. As she hunched over in her chair, she began staring in the distance and then buried her face in her hands and turned away. I heard her exasperated sighing as I watched her petite body tremble. Meanwhile, I was euphoric. Prior to Mr. Hart's explanation, I assumed I would be charged with murder and be facing a life sentence.

Still squirming, Elizabeth lifted her sweaty palms and touched the glass barrier separating the two of us. I pressed my cold, clammy hands up against hers on the other side and whispered with an empty smile, "It's going to be okay. Regardless of how much time I spend here, I will still spend eternity with you on the other side."

Our visit was almost over. As Mr. Hart was leaving, he showed me his business card. I vividly remember how it spelled out human rights:

Honorable
Upright
Moral
Authentic
Noble

Responsive
Integrity
Genuine
Honest
Tenacious
Straightforward

As he turned to walk away, I could not stop the tears from rolling down my cheeks. All I could think about as I walked back to my cell was that I was being treated fairly although I had taken a human life. He was going to ensure my human rights were upheld. I could not reconcile the fact that I still had human rights after taking the life of another human being. I wept as I walked.

Chapter 13

Hope

The next day, I had my first court hearing. As expected, bail was denied, and I was remanded to a nearby category B prison to await trial.

It was a tremendous relief knowing life in prison was off the table. Mr. Hart convinced me that most judges reduce sentences based on the defendant's level of genuine remorse. He explained other factors the court would consider when deciding the sentence included:

- Any previous convictions
- Level of cooperation with the investigation
- Whether my activity prior to the actual incident was legitimate
- My reputation/character
- If I had any severe medical conditions that required long term, urgent, or intensive treatment
- If I had a learning disability or mental disorder
- If I was the sole or primary caregiver for any dependents

Even with all that, the final decision was ultimately in the hands of the judge who had the discretion to apply whatever credit deemed appropriate. I knew Bill was dead because of me, but I didn't mean to do it.

Mr. Hart tried to convince me not to use the word *murder* anymore and strongly advised that I remove it from my vocabulary. The charge was manslaughter. Our defense strategy would be to bring to the forefront any mitigating factors that would reduce my sentence. I complied as best I could—even though, within my soul, I knew I would have to live with the guilt for the rest of my life. "God, help me!"

Less than a week after my first court appearance, Elizabeth came to visit.

"As soon as you walk free, we're going to board that flight you never got to take and head to Los Angeles where we'll start our new lives."

There was no reason to return to Tel Aviv after the business was sold or remain in London one second beyond what I had to. We started viewing this as a temporary stop on our way to making our American dreams come true.

She then told me that her parents' tour guide business had new owners. Because the sparkle in her eyes had returned, I tried my best to remain optimistic. I was excited and relieved to know she had finalized the deal. I failed miserably at trying to concentrate on something other than my own situation, but I think I conveyed a sense of superficial interest. I was thrilled that she could begin to heal and distance herself from the tragic memories left behind in Tel Aviv.

It was then that Elizabeth looked me in the face. I could see pity on her face. "You look so tattered and worn, John. Your pants are all but falling off of you."

I had probably lost at least ten pounds, but I tried to play it off. "There's such poor lighting in prison. Plus, this reflective glass barrier between us has distorted my usual handsome self."

She giggled and said, "But of course I can still see the debonaire man that I married." Then she winked at me.

For the rest of her visit, it was like none of this had ever happened. We were free to reminisce about those first days in Tel Aviv when I used to follow her around as she conducted tours. What a wonderful life we had lived, even with all the ups and downs. Our love always stood the test of time, no matter what we faced. We laughed as if we had not one care in the world for the remainder of our time together that day.

After Elizabeth left, my mood automatically shifted to defeat as I walked back to my cell with the weight of the world on my shoulders. How could I have allowed myself to end up in this horrid calamity? The worse part was that my dear sweet Elizabeth was now engulfed smack-dab in the middle of it as well.

That night, I dreamed I was at Heathrow having a delightful conversation with Bill about the gift he had purchased for his daughter. We thoroughly enjoyed each other's company until it was time to board the plane. How I wished that was how our chance encounter had taken place.

Instead, the reality was I never mumbled a single word to Bill. As we sat at the gate waiting to board our flight, I made the mistake of sitting close enough to overhear the voicemail he left his wife. I heard the excitement in his voice describing that priceless, life-changing gift he found at the Jaffa Flea Market, the same place I'd met my wife.

Perhaps because that part of the conversation had been intriguing, I paid attention a little more than I should have. I was not the eavesdropping type. I didn't meddle in anyone's business. When traveling alone, which I rarely did, I would keep to myself. What had come over me that day? I guess I'll never know.

The whole dream felt so real. I didn't realize it was a dream until I woke up. My situation flabbergasted me. Then I remembered what Mr. Hart told me during our first visit.

"Mr. Batista, I am here to support you throughout this process. I know how hard this must be for you. I will be with you every step of the way, and I can assure you I will do all within my power to secure the most reduced sentence possible. You will not spend the rest of your life in jail."

Chapter 14

Expectations and the Meltdown

At our next meeting, Mr. Hart expounded on the possible scenarios for defense: manslaughter through diminished responsibility or loss of control. When I heard the terminology, it seemed either could be logical explanations for my illogical actions. I had indeed lost control when I was in the bathroom with Bill. I was not able to explain to anyone, not even Elizabeth, what made me reach for Bill's laptop. It was *never* my intention to harm him, let alone kill him. It wasn't even my intention to take his laptop. I had not the faintest idea when Bill collapsed to the floor that he was dead. When I left the bathroom, I thought he had passed out and would be fine.

At any rate, we had possibilities. He was meeting with other colleagues at DSCC later that day to come up with a solid defense for manslaughter. Regardless of the approach, he again assured me that he felt the judge would be lenient with a reduced sentence, perhaps five to ten years.

Given the fact that I had been on medication for years, coupled with the fact that my medication had been recently changed, perhaps the judge would be even more lenient.

Sometimes I wasn't as aware of my actions as I should be. Sometimes it was hard to separate reality from irrational thoughts that tried to control my mind. Maybe that was the reason I acted so inconceivably. It rarely happened, but on occasion when I was off-balance or needed my prescriptions adjusted, *strange* things happened that were out of character for me.

Did I have a confirmed medical diagnosis? Yes, I did.

Did it fully explain why I did what I did? No, it did not. Did it contribute to my actions? Possibly.

Mr. Hart felt it needed to be mentioned so that the judge and jury would take it into consideration. If nothing else, introducing a part of me which I preferred to keep hidden may help to reduce my sentence. My numerous foster parents, guidance counselors, and social workers back in the United States all knew about it when I was growing up.

It wasn't until after Elizabeth and I were married that I was brave enough to share that information with her parents. They loved me just the same and trusted my love for their daughter far outweighed everything else. They knew I would do all in my power to love, honor, respect, and take care of their baby girl. They trusted me and knew above and beyond anything else, Elizabeth and I loved each other enough to overcome any adversity. My diagnosis usually was not an issue except when I found myself in inexplicable entanglements. This, by far, was the most dreadful predicament I had ever faced.

When Elizabeth came for her next visit, I told her all about my meeting with Mr. Hart. She had convinced herself that my court case could get dismissed. That was highly unlikely, if not impossible. I was facing involuntary manslaughter; manslaughter of any kind sounded better than murder. As much as I despised what I had done, a prison sentence of five to ten years would have been a relief. I deserved punishment. Bill's family deserved no less than that. Justice had to prevail, and that was the only way I could go on with my life—in or out of prison. Bill's family thought I would die in prison. I probably needed to do just that, but I didn't say that to Elizabeth.

As convincingly as I could, I said, "Let's talk about something else and leave the legalities to Mr. Hart."

Wiping her tears away, she nodded in agreement.

I asked how she was spending her days. She was glad to have relocated to a hotel on this side of town. It wasn't just for convenience, though. Somehow, it made her feel closer to me. She was not interested in looking for anything on a more permanent basis because she was still hoping for a dismissal.

She also did not want to return to Tel Aviv without me, but when we prepared to come to London to "confess," we'd made no preparations for an extended stay. We foolishly thought I could report what happened to the authorities, and we would be on our way back home. Elizabeth had very few belongings with her and had purchased what she needed in

London. I was in prison; hence, there was no need for any belongings.

Elizabeth made arrangements for some of her personal items and clothes to be packed and shipped to London. She said she was leaving replaceable and non-sentimental things behind for good. However, she wanted her photo albums and family mementos close to her. She was staying in a two-bedroom suite at the hotel, which was more than enough room for her immediate needs.

When our time was coming to a close, I noticed I was doing most of the talking. Elizabeth seemed a bit withdrawn and was slumped down in her chair. After I caught her staring into space, I asked what was wrong.

The floodgates opened.

She avoided looking directly into my eyes and buried her face in her hands. With heartbreak in her voice, she whispered through the tears that she could not bear to face life without me. She wasn't prepared to live five to ten years without me. She worried what would happen to me without her. I told her I was getting my medication in prison and that I was in complete control. Nothing was going to happen to me. I was prepared to face the consequences of my actions, even if it meant spending the next ten years behind bars.

"Bad people are in prison. What if they hurt you? If only I had gone to LA with you, none of this would've ever happened. You would've been talking to me at the airport and wouldn't have even overheard Bill talking on the phone."

I tried to reassure her that I would be fine, even though I had no idea how I would survive either. Nothing I said could console her. As I watched her petite body tremble in dismay, I placed my hands on the glass barrier separating us, bowed my head, closed my eyes, and began to pray.

When I opened my eyes, I found a much calmer woman sitting on the other side. Her hands were placed on the glass barrier up against mine. Her head was still bowed. As she looked up, I could see hope in her eyes.

Simultaneously, we both spoke it aloud. "Only God can save us."

Chapter 15

The Plea

My sweet Elizabeth was a ray of sunshine each time she came for a visit after that. She remained optimistic and believed that God was in control of my situation. We had lighthearted conversations, and sometimes I told her what I learned from Mr. Hart. The judicial system in London was still a mystery to me, but I trusted my solicitor. I had no other choice.

Not that I ever wanted to use my afflictions to help me escape an extended sentence, but Mr. Hart convinced me to allow medical records from Ichilov Hospital to be introduced. They helped explained what happened once I realized Bill had died. My past did not exonerate me from what I had done. I was without a doubt still guilty.

Nevertheless, after presenting the facts of the matter, Mr. Hart had somehow been able to accomplish something I thought was impossible. He said the Magistrate would understand why I pleaded guilty to the lesser charge of manslaughter. Also, my documented remorseful behavior ever since I learned the truth would make a huge impact on reducing the severity of my punishment.

When our day in court finally arrived, the Magistrate asked Mr. Hart if he wanted to present a plea in mitigation prior to the sentencing. He was brilliant. As he summarized my offense and explained the reasons behind it, he reiterated my remorse and what should be the best outcome going forward given the unique circumstances of my case.

Even though there was a mandatory minimum sentence that should be imposed, his plea no doubt influenced the Magistrate's leniency. It helped that I had no previous criminal record in the United States or Israel. My personal circumstances from childhood in addition to challenges I faced as an adult also played a major part in his plea.

Elizabeth and I held our breath as the sentence was announced.

"John Batista, you are sentenced to two years in prison."

I gasped. The weight of the world vanished from my shoulders. While I felt I deserved life in prison, what I was guilty of was an accident. The Magistrate was convinced of that. I was expecting at least five years even after Mr. Hart explained how he intended to plead for leniency. I had not forgiven myself for what I had done, yet I was granted compassion and mercy.

I turned around in awe, and there was Elizabeth—in the front row with a wide-eyed stare on her face. She didn't blink until tears dropped off her chin.

Her body language usually gave her away, but this time I couldn't read her. They escorted me from the room without allowing us an opportunity to talk.

I left the courtroom not knowing if she was okay.

While the court proceedings were quick and simple, I knew Mr. Hart had pulled off a marvelous feat. What was most concerning to me at that particular moment was my wife. Once I made it back to my prison cell, I began praying for her. I had been praying for her for weeks prior to the court date. Now, it was different. All of the legalities were over. I knew my fate and was prepared to accept it.

I was relieved but troubled. The only thoughts floating around in my mind for the rest of that day centered around Elizabeth. I dreamed about her that night. She was aimlessly wandering the streets of London all day. By nightfall, she had walked nineteen miles from Heathrow Airport to London Bridge. She appeared confused at first, but then she realized she needed to walk on the other side of the security barriers reserved for pedestrians.

Midway across the bridge, she stopped. She sat down on the pavement, crossed her legs, and bowed her head as if she was praying. After a few minutes, she jumped up, got a running start, and leaped over the guard rail into the Thames River. A strong current immediately swept her away.

Awakening with a jolt, I found myself on the cold, concrete floor, thrashing about as if I was swimming fiercely. It took me a few moments to realize I was still in prison and not in the icy river desperately trying to rescue Elizabeth. I pleaded with God to allow my darling wife to be safe and sound at the hotel.

Chapter 16

Embrace the Future

Mr. Hart came to visit early the next morning, soon after that disturbing nightmare sent me on a crazy tangent. My first question to him was if he had talked to Elizabeth. As a matter of fact, he had spoken to her a few minutes prior. He said the officials confirmed with him that I would serve out the rest of my sentence at that same prison. He informed Elizabeth of that right before he came in to see me. She told him that she would be scheduling a visit as soon as possible now that sentencing was over.

Whew! What a relief. I knew where Elizabeth was, and she was safe.

After explaining all the details of what to expect from that point moving forward, we completed the necessary legalities. I thanked him for all he had done for me and my wife. Then he wished me well and assured me he was a mere phone call away. I found myself breathing much easier as I watched him leave.

Two years. I could endure this for two years. It would make Elizabeth and me stronger in the end.

Then I thought about Bill Williams's family. He'd found his daughter a priceless treasure for her birthday, and now she'd never receive it. Had she even been able to celebrate her birthday? Or had it come with the news that her father had been found dead in an airport bathroom?

The relief I felt was crushed under the weight of that reality. Even though I would not have to spend the rest of my life behind bars, I recognized that I would be tormented by my own internal prison for which there would be no end. My prison sentence was only two years of my life, but the lives of Mrs. Williams and her daughter had been shattered.

How I wished I could apologize and make amends. There was nothing I could do or say to make their lives better. I'm fairly certain they wished I was dead. Sometimes I wished I was dead too. It would have taken away the painful reality of what I had done. Perhaps the finality of meeting with Mr. Hart caused me to become more reflective. I could hardly stand to even think about the Williams family. It was much too agonizing trying to put myself in their shoes. I was barely able to stand in my own.

As the next few days passed, I adjusted more to the prison schedule and tried to focus on the fact that this was a temporary situation. Bill never had a chance. His family would have to live the rest of their lives without him. Yet I was given the luxury of only altering my life for a mere two years. My mind meandered from one extreme to the other. Most times, when I thought about Elizabeth, I would also think about Grace.

Much to my surprise, when the guard called me later that week to say I had a visitor, I was escorted to a different area and told to have a seat. This room had no glass barriers. Instead, they had "prison visit tables" which would be where Elizabeth and I would visit from there on out. When I saw her enter the room, I couldn't sit still. She had a radiant glow about her. It was as if I was in college again and seeing her for the very first time. She had not aged in over twenty years. She captured my heart way back then and never let go. In her, I could put my trust, my life, my very reason for existence.

Before realizing what I was doing, I jumped up from my seat and ran toward her. With no glass barrier separating us, all I wanted was to embrace her and never let go. I *needed* to feel her, and I did.

"*Batista!* Get back in your seat, *now!*"

The guard drew his baton and banged it on the table.

"Please forgive me. That will never happen again."

I was thinking if I ever got the chance, I would do it again… and again… and again… It would be worth the baton-beating. Then I came to my senses and succumbed to reality. I did not want to mess up anything that could possibly delay my release or prevent Elizabeth from visiting as often as possible.

I apologized profusely as I regained composure back in my chair.

The only thing the guard uttered back was that it better not happen again or they would suspend my visitation privileges indefinitely.

As Elizabeth was taking her seat, she tossed her lovely locks away from her face. I locked in on her beautiful brown eyes. She winked and then fluttered those long lashes. At that moment, all was right with the world. After we were both sitting at the table, I asked the guard if we were allowed to hold hands on top of it. He said we could.

For that entire one-hour visit, our hands were intertwined. I caressed her thumb with mine. She caressed my pinky finger with hers. This felt better than our first date!

We talked about our plans for surviving the next two years. Elizabeth said she would like to briefly return to Tel Aviv, just to go through some personal items. She had already sold her parents' home after they passed. Their important belongings and sentimental items were at our home. Some items were in storage.

She also wanted to pack some things herself to bring back to London. While there, she would make plans to sell our home. This would be her final trip to Tel Aviv and would take about a week to wrap up everything. She had also began looking for a permanent place to live in London for the next two years.

I asked Elizabeth what was she going to do in London for the next two years. She had no idea and said she had not thought about it. All she could focus on right then was finalizing things in Tel Aviv and then finding a place to call home in London. After settling in, then she would decide how to occupy her time with something other than waiting for the next time she could come visit me.

Even with all the uncertainties, it looked as if everything was going to work out fine.

If only I had known what the future held.

Chapter 17

You've Got Mail

Elizabeth returned from Tel Aviv having accomplished all she had set out to do. That was it. She had no plans to ever return to her homeland again. She soon settled into a modest condominium in London in what was considered a very safe part of town. It wasn't that far from the prison, which somehow still made her feel closer to me.

Having no desire to start a new life in London without me, she didn't get out much, nor did she try to meet new people. Her sole purpose at that point was to endure the life-shattering predicament that had befallen us. She kept to herself most of the time, but she did enjoy going to the park when the weather permitted.

During one visit, she told me she was struggling with finding ways to cope with our new reality. She decided to do some research in hopes of connecting with other women facing similar conundrums. Her internet search pulled up a local support group, but she never contacted them; she wasn't interested in meeting anyone in person, let alone a whole group. What interested her the most was an online support group based out of the United States.

I found it quite interesting of all the online resources, she would be attracted to a group in America. Nevertheless, I was thrilled that something had grabbed her attention. Being powerless to change our circumstances, I wanted nothing more than for Elizabeth to find peace and the strength to endure what was a prison sentence for her too.

When she first joined the online group, she remained inconspicuous. She would read the posts and comments but never chimed in. She found solace in others' conversations. Within a month of joining, she had a much better perspective. It was the comfort she needed at the time.

Meanwhile, there was no comfort to be found in prison. I was counting down the seven hundred thirty days of mental and physical confinement. I made do as best I could. I started reading to pass the time of day.

There were times when I doubted our marriage would survive. My biggest fear was that Elizabeth would grow weary of waiting for me. I loved that woman with my whole heart. Deep down, I knew she felt the same about me, as she had proven it over and over again throughout our marriage. We had faced trials and tribulations before, but this was by far the most irrational thing I had ever done. Worries tormented me. What if our separation became too much for her to endure?

Roughly four months into this harrowing prison ordeal, Elizabeth sat with me at the visitor's table. As usual, our fingers were intertwined while we caressed each other. She told me that she had started journaling as a way to express her emotions. She was in a better space. That made my space better also.

It was during that particular visit that she reassured me that her love for me had never changed. As a matter of fact, she said that, through journaling, she had been able to explore her feelings and emotions on a different level. What surprised me the most was her next statement.

"My dearest John, I have come to realize that there is no true definition of love. It's impossible to define what is indescribable. This one thing I know: you are the absolute love of my life. You always have been, and you always will be. God put the purest form of love in my heart for you, and nothing will ever change that. With every breath I take, I breathe more love for you."

At that moment, I felt closer to my wife than ever before. I looked down at our locked hands. Our fingernails were pale. We were squeezing each other so tightly that we cut off the circulation in our hands. I sobbed the happiest silent cry ever.

Things were never the same after that visit. My joy returned. My peace returned. My Elizabeth and her undying love for me had returned, although I realized it never left. I think I became the happiest incarcerated man on earth. Still, I counted down the days until I was set free. It was my prayer that somehow Bill's family would also be able to find a sense of peace and find a way to carry on with their lives.

The next few months seemed to accelerate in time. I'm not sure, but I think about seven or eight months had passed since they whisked me off that airplane. Under the circumstances, I could not have expected my life to be going any better than it was. Yes, I had been convicted of manslaughter. Yes, I was guilty. Yes, I had Bill's blood on my hands, albeit not literally but definitely figuratively. And yes, I was more remorseful than mere words could describe.

But I was okay.

I was okay until I received mail. It was the first time I had ever gotten mail in prison. I had seen some of the other inmates get letters, mainly those who never had any visitors. Elizabeth came every time, like clockwork, and always utilized the visitor's schedule to the maximum every week. It was the sole reason for her move to London, so she could be closer to me and visit at every opportunity. There was no reason for me to get any mail because there was no one else who loved or missed me.

"Batista! You've got mail."

It was the beginning of a monumental meltdown.

Chapter 18

Boy, Oh Boy!

I had no idea who would be contacting me by mail, so needless to say, when I saw the envelope's return address was from Grace Williams in Los Angeles, I panicked.

Actually, I did more than panic. I hyperventilated. My heart raced. My fingers went numb. My toes started tingling. I was lightheaded. My vision blurred. My head pounded. I was in my cell all alone and had to focus to regain my composure. I could not let myself have another seizure.

Of course, the envelope had already been opened in the mailroom before being distributed. I sat on that cold, hard cot, contemplating the content inside the envelope. I must have stared at it thirty minutes before pulling out the letter.

Once it was in my hands, my world started moving in slow motion. As I unfolded the paper inside, I saw there were multiple pages. Without looking at the words, I counted seven handwritten pages. Behind those pages were several typed pages, some containing pictures and other details. I had no idea what it all meant, and I was afraid to begin reading. I thought about what it must have taken for Bill's wife to pen such a letter. I held my breath and through the tears and blurred vision, I dove into the letter.

It was an out-of-body experience. I saw myself sitting on the cot reading the letter. Yet I could feel every single word with every belabored breath I took. Eventually, I witnessed myself reach page seven. Her very last sentence on that page began to echo in my mind.

"Bill's legacy will live on through our precious baby boy, William Matthew Williams III."

"Bill's legacy will live on through our precious baby boy, William Matthew Williams III."

"Bill's legacy will live on through our precious baby boy, William Matthew Williams III."

Elizabeth and I named our only child, who perished during childbirth, Matthew!

I wept.

I wailed.

I wept and wailed.

I woke up in solitary confinement and found myself bound in a straitjacket. Thus, my dear, imaginary friends, this is how my story unfolded. Reading that brutally honest letter from Grace opened up past wounds I thought were buried. It hit me differently knowing Bill would never know his child, and that child would never know his father. My son never knew me either.

For the past twenty years, not a day had passed that I did not think about my own precious baby boy. I never heard him cry, yet the tears he had left behind for Elizabeth and I to wipe never ended. He never took a single, solitary breath—yet with every breath Elizabeth and I fought to take on that god-awful day, we found no comfort or will to continue living. It was categorically the absolute worst day of my human existence, and I left the hospital mad at the world and everything in it except for my precious wife. I adored her even more after witnessing all that she suffered for naught.

That raw letter was no doubt what I needed to read. After all, I was guilty, and I suspected that Bill's wife would never forgive me. I had been praying for her family ever since I realized what I had done. I wanted the Williams family to find peace and joy in their lives again.

Grace's forgiveness of my sin and redemption of my soul was something I could not accept at that moment. Emotions I'd suppressed for twenty years after losing Matthew, coupled with the emotional roller coaster I had been on was too much to bear. Hence, my total meltdown ensued. Now that I reflect on that abysmal day, I know why I needed the straightjacket.

Lying there still bound in solitary confinement, replaying all those details and telling my story to an invisible audience was cathartic. I felt better afterward and stopped talking to myself. I drifted off to a deep sleep, only to be awakened by two apprehensive officers calling my name. They came into the padded room with a man wearing a white lab jacket.

"Good evening, Mr. Batista. I'm Dr. Gray, a psychologist on staff here. How are you today?"

"Much better," I replied.

That precipitous letter from Grace let the genie out of the bottle. As honest and straightforward as she had been, I had to be honest with myself and face my fears. What a perfect name. Grace was indeed *grace*, personified. She extended grace that I surely did not deserve.

Dr. Gray and the two officers soon realized that I had calmed all the way down. No more weeping. No more wailing. I had come to terms with everything.

Everything.

One of the officers untied the straightjacket while the other offered me water. Dr. Gray instructed them to escort me to the conference room where we could sit and talk in a more comfortable environment. There was no need to restrain me. I was in full control and presented no threat of harm to myself or anyone else.

We actually had quite a lovely chat. I told him about the letter, not knowing he had already seen it. When I lost control and had to be bound and whisked away, a guard took possession of the letter and turned it over to his supervisor. When they called in Dr. Gray to do a mental evaluation, they showed him the letter. They also gave him all the pertinent details about my case before he ever laid eyes on me in solitary confinement.

Even though he worked for the prison system, I found myself more comfortable talking to him than any of my previous psychologists and psychiatrists. I'd had my fair share of both, starting in early childhood when I first began my journey in the foster care system back home in America. He also knew of my diagnosis after reviewing my medical records and saw the list of medications that I took on a regular basis.

Exhibiting no preconceived notions of what one might categorize as a hopeless case, Dr. Gray was who I needed to talk to at that pivotal moment. I appreciated his understanding and asked if he thought it would be okay for them to release the letter back to me. I hadn't been able to read the extra material Grace included with her letter. He thought it would be better for him to be present, just in case. He said he would schedule another visit in a couple of days now that the emergent situation had concluded.

I spent about an hour with Dr. Gray that day. When he left, I began to reflect on Grace's redemptive letter and the strength it must have taken to write it. I assumed she had given birth before the letter reached me. If she'd been due any day while writing the letter, she'd surely already given birth.

William Matthew Williams, III, her miracle child.

Bill's legacy would live on.

My thoughts turned once more to Elizabeth and our baby. We adored Matthew from the day we found out she was expecting. I began to relive those glorious months of anticipation waiting for his birth. We bonded with him in utero. I felt him move inside her. I saw his heart beating on the ultrasound. I witnessed my wife's transformation to motherhood.

The squeaking of my cell door startled me. A guard brought my dinner, which I had missed while in solitary confinement.

Perhaps it was for the best. I have a feeling the picture ingrained in my mind of Elizabeth holding Matthew's lifeless body against her bosom was about to set off a volcanic eruption of suppressed tears.

Instead, I scarfed down that miserable dinner and fell asleep. I don't recall that I had a dream at all that night. My sleep was sweet.

Chapter 19

Grace

I was relieved that Elizabeth wasn't scheduled for a visit until after I saw the psychologist again, giving me time to process all that had occurred. For the next couple days, I went about my regular routine. I assumed Dr. Gray had given clearance for me to remain in the general population. As much as I abhorred mingling with the other prisoners, I had gotten used to it. It was better than solitary confinement.

Without access to Grace's letter, it was difficult to remember all she had said. I will never forget the gist of her letter, though, and that was what I reflected on during my quiet time. The most hurtful part was her confession that she wanted me to suffer with every breath I took. She hoped all my days and nights would be filled with tormenting pictures of Bill's lifeless body lying on the floor. She even said that it would have made her deliriously happy to hear that I took my own life or that some other prisoner did to me what I did to Bill.

That was heartless—yet I understood her pain.

Had I been in her shoes, I would have felt the same.

How thankful I am that she was able to work through all that anguish and inner turmoil. She said it was only because of God's love, his grace, and his mercy that she was able to forgive me. She prayed for me and wanted me to find peace with what I had done. She even said that God himself wanted to forgive me. As uncomfortable and rattled as I was reading the letter, that part about forgiveness I remembered verbatim.

"As a matter of fact, God wants to forgive you. All you have to do is ask. Then you can have peace right here on earth and eternal life with him in heaven. I discovered over these past few months of grieving my insuperable loss that I did not have peace in my mind. By forgiving you and sending this letter, I am now free. I can move forward with a renewed spirit and joy in my life again."

What a remarkable woman!

What a wonderful wife she must have been. Oh, how much she must have loved her husband. And what a terrible and profound loss I forced her to endure. Yet, she wanted me to make peace with God.

I prayed.

She prayed.

I wondered for a brief moment if we were praying to the same God.

I did an enormous amount of soul-searching while waiting in great anticipation for Dr. Gray's next visit. I wanted to see Grace's letter more than I wanted to see him. While I struggled to accept her unparalleled compassion and forgiveness, I found myself not nearly as curious as I thought I would be about finding out more about what started this whole nightmarish situation—the birthday gift.

She said it was some kind of sculpture of the Gospel Symbol. It was intriguing, but I couldn't quite remember how she explained what the sculpture meant. She thought it would change my life, though. That, I did remember. Bill had told her in the voicemail that it was priceless and life-changing. It had proven to be both—in that Bill gave his life for it.

When Dr. Gray came for his second visit, we met in the health and safety room. One guard was also present.

"Good morning, Mr. Batista. I trust you are doing even better today. Let's talk about what happened when you read that letter from Grace Williams."

I explained to Dr. Gray that it was a two-fold reaction. First and foremost was the fact that I had to acknowledge I murdered—or as they called it, manslaughtered—the innocent husband of a devoted wife who was now expecting a child they never thought they would conceive. His middle name was Matthew, the same name that Elizabeth and I named our one and only child who died during childbirth, crushing all our hopes and dreams.

That in itself sounded like an incredibly tall and implausible tale. Who would believe such a preposterous story? Yet I was entangled right in the middle of it.

Secondly, it was quite troubling that Grace was so full of grace that she forgave me for taking Bill's life and destroying hers. Not only did she forgive me, but she prayed that I could accept the fact that God wanted to forgive me as well.

How could she forgive me, and why would God want to forgive me?

"So, you see, Dr. Gray, not only was I not expecting a letter at all, but upon reading the content, it was too much for me to bear. As they say, it sent me over the deep end. Grace's unmerited grace toward me was more than I could accept."

We proceeded to talk about my reaction and how best to deal with those emotions. I had already heard most of what he said from previous mental health counseling sessions anyway. It's one thing to know how I should respond and quite a different situation to be able to respond like I should when faced with what appears to be insurmountable adversities at the time.

I grew tired of *therapy* after a few minutes. We only had one hour, and I was anxious to review that letter. Although I could appreciate Dr. Gray's efforts to help me work through my emotions, all I wanted from that visit was to be cleared to take possession of the letter from Grace. Since he was the one in charge, I remained calm and followed his lead. Eventually, he pulled the letter out of the folder he had lying on the table.

"Mr. Batista, let's take a look at this letter more carefully. Are you ready to proceed?"

"Yes sir, Dr. Gray! I'm ready… I am ready!"

He began cautiously. Soon, it was apparent that I had gotten my emotions under control. I was not about to blow that opportunity. After reading it the second time, I understood why my raw reaction a couple of days prior was so profound and extreme.

Then he asked if I had read the two supplemental documents when the letter first arrived. I had not. I caught a glimpse of the other information, which appeared to be much more formal documents. They were typed and had pictures scattered throughout. I did not have a clue as to what was included except it had something to do with explaining the sculpture Bill found and what it meant.

Dr. Gray went on to explain he read the attachments and found them quite intriguing. He asked if I was a man of faith. I explained that while growing up, some of my foster parents took me to church. Others did not.

I never gave it much thought, but if asked, I would have classified myself as a Christian. I was just as much a Christian as anyone else in America. I believed God existed; thus, I had faith.

Unsure how much of my past he already knew, I went on to explain that I was an international student from the United States enrolled at Tel Aviv University as part of a study abroad program. That's where I met Elizabeth. After spending a year in Israel, I returned home, graduated from college, and made preparations to relocate to Tel Aviv so that I could marry Elizabeth.

To get permission from her parents to marry their daughter, I converted to Judaism and never looked back.

It was at that point in our conversation that Dr. Gray agreed to leave Grace's letter and attachments with me. He said he understood why my initial reaction to the letter was so bizarre and that he felt sure I was much more prepared to deal with the details now. He had no hesitation about giving me all the contents inside the envelope. He cautioned me that the supplemental information may be confusing at first because it represented a Christian point of view.

His strongest recommendation was to proceed with caution due to the sensitive nature of conflicting religious beliefs. The topic was not something that would send me over the edge, though. All of that seemed minor compared to the emotional trauma of reading Grace's letter the first time.

Dr. Gray assured me he was available to talk should I ever feel uncomfortable about anything. He wanted me to feel safe and secure and to avoid any type of emotional dilemma or decline in my mental health status. He said he would schedule a two-week follow up meeting to check in with me. In the meantime, if I needed to talk before then, he said I could notify a guard. My record would be marked that he was on call for me as needed.

I thanked him for showing such kindness and compassion. As he was leaving, I asked if he was comfortable in sharing what his religious beliefs were. He laughed and said he was the son of a prominent Protestant pastor in the United Kingdom.

Enough said…

Chapter 20

The Attachments

After Dr. Gray left, I read the letter from Grace multiple times and found great comfort in it. Then I tackled the two attachments. One was brief. Quite literally, it was a breakdown of John 3:16 with pictures explaining different parts of the verse. How shocking to realize the priceless, life-changing gift that Bill told Grace about was a beautiful sculpture of what he called the Gospel Symbol. It was a visual presentation of John 3:16! (Refer to the *Afterword* for a full explanation.)

Reading the explanation behind that verse gave me great reason to pause. It gave me chills. I had never seen a symbolic presentation of what John 3:16 means.

I had gone to church whenever my foster parents took me. One home that I lived in had two other foster children there at the same time. We adored that elderly couple, but I only had the benefit of being with them from ages ten to fourteen. During those four years, I had read the entire Bible from Genesis to Revelation. When Papa Beard took sick, Mama Beard was no longer able to care for us because she had to take care of him. I was sent to a different home where those foster parents did not go to church. I never saw the other two children again.

Throughout my childhood, I had been in and out of various foster homes and group homes, all of which had different views of Christianity. By the time I enrolled in college, religion wasn't on my radar, but I did own a Bible, which I read from time to time. I believed God created… just as Genesis 1:1 says. However, I was focused on the whole college experience and was more concerned with obtaining my degree and becoming successful in my chosen profession.

When I had fallen in love with Elizabeth, the choice to convert to Judaism was easy because that was the only way I could marry her. Religious leaders advised to never convert for the sole reason of getting married. I understood that, but I was devoted to her, which made me devoted to her religion as well. The process was long but well worth it. I was happy and content with my choices.

Now I was reading John 3:16 again, which I had not done since leaving America at the age of twenty-one.

When I made it to the more detailed attachment, I

discovered it was much more in-depth and comprehensive. It went into a lengthy explanation about what the Gospel Symbol represented. I studied all those pages for quite some time, trying to get a full understanding of what the Gospel Symbol meant. (Refer to the *Afterword* for this detailed explanation.)

It was overwhelming, yet it spoke to my heart. I reflected on the time I spent with the elderly couple and beliefs I had then that had long since been repressed. I thought about Grace and the faith she must have had to even want to share that information with me. At the time she sent it, she thought I was a cruel, cold-blooded murderer, yet she felt that God wanted to forgive me and reward me with eternal life, if I believed. It was a great deal to take in all at once. I studied the information and prayed about it all day.

In my dream that night, I could hear Grace saying that I needed Christ in my life. She had no idea if I was a believer or not, but she probably assumed I wasn't because she thought I was a cold-blooded killer. She told me in the dream, just as she had written in the letter, that it was not too late for me to have a covenant relationship with Jesus. She prayed for me to accept Jesus Christ as my Lord and Savior.

I woke up the following morning feeling peaceful and refreshed. Elizabeth was scheduled to visit that day, but for the time being, I chose not to tell her anything about the letter nor about my experience in solitary confinement. It would have caused her a great deal of agony, so I spared her of those details.

We had a lovely visit, having grown accustomed to this

horrible situation and separation. At least I could feel her next to me, even though there was no privacy in the visitation room. Conjugal visits were not allowed. We trusted each other and remained committed to our marriage. Holding her hands was as close to caressing her body as I could get. Yet when I gazed into her eyes, I felt closer than ever. Elizabeth was indeed the best thing that ever happened to me!

After she left, I went back to the letter. In the prison library, I started researching different approaches for how Christians witness to Jews. I thought that would help me work through the conflicts I was having between what I was taught as a child and what I had grown to embrace being married to a sweet Jewish woman. At this point, I was just glad that Elizabeth's parents had held more conservative views of Judaism. Elizabeth was even more conservative and did not hold on to orthodox beliefs at all.

With Grace proclaiming faith in the sacrificial work of Jesus on the cross, I couldn't help but wonder if she would have found the grace to forgive me without her beliefs. I did not have to "work" for her forgiveness. She freely gave it, just as Christianity taught that Jesus freely gave his life to save us from our sin. Needless to say, I needed to be forgiven of my sin.

What I learned pouring through resources in the library is that many Christians are afraid to witness to Jewish people for fear of us rejecting Jesus as the Messiah and instead holding fast to the belief that he is a moral teacher with no claims to deity. I did not want Elizabeth to feel that I was suddenly rejecting her heritage and beliefs after over twenty years.

My research took me to several Messianic passages in the Bible. I won't dwell on them now. Suffice it to say, I found many compelling scriptures that Jesus is the Messiah. It was his atoning work of sacrifice that could bring me into a right relationship with God. It was just like that second attachment Grace sent me that was labeled critical information. It said, "The most important message God has ever given to the people of the world is the Gospel of Jesus Christ. Because in him, and only him, we are in relationship with God."

"Jesus said to him, I am the way, and the truth, and the life. No one comes to the Father except through me" (John 14:6).

The longer I researched, the more compelling the evidence.

Grace Williams extended unmerited grace toward me. I did not deserve her forgiveness. I found it hard to believe that God *wanted* to forgive me. During the peak of my turmoil, I thought I was going to rot in jail and then rot in hell. The judge granted leniency. Two years of my life was a small price to pay for taking someone else's life.

I ran across another Bible verse during my research: "For by grace are ye saved through faith; and that not of yourselves; it is the gift of God" (Ephesians 2:8).

As I meditated and researched that particular Bible verse, I remembered Grace Williams had that same verse on the bottom of her stationery.

That was my answer!

I was redeemed!

Grace saved me!

Chapter 21

Pay It Forward

As I pondered more deeply about Grace Williams's letter, I began reflecting on what the expression "Pay it Forward" means. It describes the beneficiary of a good deed repaying the kindness to others instead of to the original benefactor.

Grace Williams was my benefactor. She had forgiven me, thus allowing me to forgive myself. She reintroduced me to John 3:16, and now I have a covenant relationship with my Lord and Savior, Jesus Christ.

I will never be able to repay her for the kindness and compassion she showed me in that letter. I doubt she would ever want to hear from me at all. However, I did write back to her. I don't know if she will even open the envelope when she sees it is from me, but I pray that she will. I wrote it believing she will.

Being more remorseful than I could ever put into words, I explained what happened in the bathroom at Heathrow and why. Profusely apologizing for my mistake and what appeared to be two weeks of running and hiding, I told her why things appeared to be a certain way when reality was something much different. I did not want to make the letter sound as if I did not take ownership of what I had done or that I was making excuses. I kept it brief but wanted her to know what happened. She more than deserved that.

The rest of the letter was to thank her for sharing the Gospel Message with me. I told her that I was now a born-again believer, having accepted Jesus Christ as my Savior. I was thrilled to welcome my Redeemer into my heart. I assured her that I was paying it forward also. Although I could not repay her kindness, I was committed to sharing it with others.

About two months after receiving Grace's letter, I started my own prison ministry. I shared the Gospel Message with anyone who would listen to me, guards and inmates alike. It didn't matter who. When given the opportunity, I shared my testimony and John 3:16 boldly, yet discretely. After all, I was in prison for manslaughter and wanted to fulfill my two-year sentence without incident so that I could be released into Elizabeth's arms. Meanwhile, I wanted to honor Grace because her outreach had not fallen on deaf ears. She was responsible for many souls being saved within the confines of that London prison.

What became even more unbelievable is that Elizabeth converted from Judaism to Christianity. At first, I was afraid to share Grace's letter with her, but I eventually did. She could see the monumental change in me before I told her what happened. Because I believed that God sent his Son to die on the cross to save not only me, but whoever believes, that helped her to accept Jesus as the Messiah and her Savior. It wasn't an instantaneous transformation. Quite naturally, this came as a surprise when she first heard me speak of it. Judaism was all she had known her entire life.

I did not pressure her, but instead trusted the Gospel Message would speak for itself. She pondered it for several weeks and did her own soul-searching for answers. It had to be her personal decision. The day she came to visit after making her own covenant relationship with Jesus was the happiest day of my life! When I saw her walk in the room that day, she was glowing more radiantly than our wedding day. Straightaway, I knew my prayers had been answered.

Our newfound happiness and unspeakable joy amidst a terrible situation continued for several months. My first year of imprisonment seemed to fly by much quicker than I imagined. Elizabeth even became active in the local support group for wives of inmates. She visited a church one of the other wives attended and found her safe haven.

I celebrated in her joyous announcement that she joined the church. Never in my wildest imagination would I have believed one day I would be in a London prison for manslaughter running a prison ministry, spreading the good news of Jesus Christ while my wife became an active member of London Christian Fellowship Church. My truth became better than any fictional story of grace and redemption.

Making good of a bad situation had proven to be life-changing for me. As I ministered to others, I often thought about Bill Williams and his description of the priceless, life-changing gift he found for his daughter. That beautiful sculpture had changed my life as well. My endeavor was to share that message wherever I went. Elizabeth and I even made plans for how we could continue sharing that message once my two years were up.

We were moving to the United States. My preference was Los Angeles, but out of respect for Grace Williams, we decided on San Francisco instead. The cities were almost four hundred miles apart, a six-hour drive. Elizabeth and I did not think our paths would ever cross with Grace. I'm sure she never wanted to lay eyes on me. We would start a non-profit organization to share the Gospel Message in the prisons encompassing the Bay Area.

First things first, though, as I only had about six months left on my sentence. My cellmate had been telling me about conversations he overheard between some prisoners and guards. All were not happy that I was spreading the Gospel. Some were angry that I had the audacity to share such hope. I remained discrete and sensitive of others who may not have wanted to hear what I was sharing. I even discussed it with Dr. Gray, who still came to visit. He cautioned me but saw my enthusiasm could not be shaken. I had been set free while in prison and wanted others to experience that same freedom.

One day in the yard, while standing on the sideline watching some fellows play basketball, I witnessed a brutal situation that escalated to a moment of terror. While arguing over a minor altercation, one prisoner pulled out a makeshift knife and stabbed another prisoner in the stomach and chest.

As he was falling to the ground, he grabbed him by the neck and began choking him. The guards broke up the situation, likely saving the man's life.

That wasn't the first time I had witnessed violence in prison. It was commonplace to see fights break out, but most did not involve weapons. I was amazed whenever I saw knives and other illegal paraphernalia, but it was always a known fact that these sorts of things occurred behind bars. Meanwhile, I kept a low profile and tried my best to stay out of trouble while counting down the days.

With just a few months before I was set free, Elizabeth had begun planning for our move to San Francisco. We wanted to be productive as soon as we got there. We even came up with a name for our nonprofit organization, ***Grace: Pay It Forward.***

Life was good inside those prison walls. I found my Savior, and I was going to spend the rest of my life, whether it be long or short, paying it forward.

Chapter 22

Regret and Sufficiency

"**M**rs. Batista, I regret to inform you that your husband was found lying in the shower…"

I yelled at the prison official who was talking in slow motion at my front door. "Don't you dare say another word! Leave right now! Just go! Please just go away!"

I knew he couldn't.

As much as I wished he would disappear, his face is etched in my mind. Whether he audibly finished the sentence or not, I knew how it was going to end but could not bear to listen. I fell to my knees, gasping for air. There was no life left in me. Then he said it again, the most abominable words I could never unhear.

"Mrs. Batista, I regret to inform you that your husband was found lying in the shower unresponsive. They tried to save him, but it was too late."

My heart shattered inside my body, making it impossible to put back together. Unable to stand, I felt the officer lift me up, carry me inside the condo, and place me on the sofa as I sobbed. I have no idea how long this went on as time seemed to have stopped.

Eventually I heard him ask, "Mrs. Batista, is there anything I can do for you or anyone I can call?"

There was nothing he could do.

I had no one he could call.

My life was over.

John took it with him.

I finally managed to ask, "Did he slip and hit his head? What happened?" It didn't matter what his response was. The outcome was still the same, regardless of how the accident happened.

He said something about the Prisons and Probation Ombudsman carrying out an independent investigation as required by law when anyone in custody dies for any reason. He said they would figure out what happened to try to make it safer for others.

Others? I didn't care about others. All I knew was that my precious husband was gone. What were they going to do? Install non-slip shower mats? John had told me about the poor, unsanitary conditions of the communal shower. They were horrid, and he hated using them. There wasn't anything left to be said or done.

I told the officer there wasn't anything I needed and that I would be fine, but I was simply trying to get him out of my house pronto. I could not tolerate his presence any longer. He gave me his card and said I could call him anytime. As he was leaving, he said someone would call me before the end of the day with additional details about how to claim John's body.

The door closed.

I wept.

I wailed.

I wept and wailed.

I lay on my sofa, weeping and wailing until I fell asleep.

That night, I dreamed about John and Matthew. At first, John was holding Matthew in his arms like a newborn baby. He looked just like he did when he was lying in the bassinette at the hospital. As the dream continued, Matthew was as tall as John, but he still had a newborn's face. Near the end of my sweet dream, Matthew looked just like his daddy the first time I laid eyes on him. The two of them were walking side-by-side down a street paved with gold. Their arms were crossed over each other's shoulders, and their steps were in perfect unison. It was the most beautiful sight I had ever seen in my life. The joy and peace on their faces made me want to join them.

I awakened and realized it had been a dream. Then I remembered John 3:16. It wasn't a dream after all! I was assured of that. John was able to behold his living, breathing baby boy in heaven. My two loves had eternal life! Grieving miserably, I found solace in the midst of my raging storm.

Later that morning, Dr. Gray called. He asked if he could meet with me in a couple of hours. John respected him a great deal and often told me how much he valued his visits and friendship. I had no one else to turn to, so I welcomed his visit.

Meanwhile, I couldn't help but reflect on the dream I had about John and Matthew. It started to mend my brokenness. John had loved that baby from the moment we found out we were expecting. Not ever knowing his biological father made John even more committed to being the best father he could be. During the ultrasound, I saw his face light up like the morning sun when my doctor announced the baby's gender.

We decided to name him Matthew because it stemmed from the Hebrew name Mattityahu, which means *gift of Yahweh*, or *gift of God*. Matthew itself means *gift*, although some say it means *gift of God*, or even *gift from God*. Interestingly, now that I am a Christian, it's even more poignant because the Biblical Matthew was the apostle who wrote the first Gospel in the New Testament.

Oh, how my heart was shattered into millions of pieces.

How I longed to hold my baby boy, and how I longed for John to hold us both.

While waiting for Dr. Gray to arrive, I couldn't help but reflect on my loneliness. We had lost Matthew twenty years prior. John had been my rock during the most horrific day of my life. We had arrived at the hospital after my water broke with everything going as expected. I had been in labor for about seven hours with no cause for alarm. They had checked me frequently and assured me that Matthew was doing well.

Suddenly, something happened. Alarms started going off. In the blink of an eye, the best day of my life had become an absolute nightmare. My doctor said they were going to have to perform an emergency Caesarean section because Matthew's heart rate had plummeted for inexplicable reasons. No matter what they tried, it would not come back up. I was only five centimeters dilated, but they had to get him out immediately. During all of the commotion, my heart rate plummeted also, and I passed out. When I awakened, John was in bed with me.

He leaned over and whispered in my ear that we lost the baby. The only reason I did not fall apart at that very moment was because John was holding me just that tight. He held me and would not let go. I buried my head in his chest and tried my best to breathe. I was being comforted by the strongest man I know. He wiped my tears away because I had not the strength to do so myself. I felt paralyzed.

John had asked them to leave Matthew in the room until I awakened. He was in the bassinette which John had turned the other way so I could not see inside. He told me everything that had happened and how they tried to save him. It wasn't meant to be. Our precious little Matthew had perished at birth. John estimated he had been able to hold him for nearly thirty minutes before the nurses said they needed to do what they needed to do.

Letting go of him was excruciating for John. They had given me medication to regulate my body and bring my vital signs back to normal. It had been about an hour after I passed out before I awakened. The nurses had cleaned up Matthew and dressed him in the cute little outfit he was going to wear home from the hospital. John asked if I was ready to see my baby. With tears rolling down my face like a waterfall, I said yes.

He went to the bassinette and cradled Matthew as he picked him up. Ever so gently, he brought him over to me and placed him on my chest. Then he got back in bed and cradled me.

I had to stay overnight to ensure I was stable for discharge. John never left my side. He did all that was humanly possible to comfort me while grieving the loss just as profoundly as I. My doctor also said we would not be able to have any more children. The irreparable damage was done. Our dreams were dead.

Going home without Matthew the next day was the

hardest thing I ever had to do. My parents had been waiting at our home when we arrived. They took care of everything and just let us exist. Through it all, I saw John's strength like never before. He was my rock, my superhero. If he could have breathed for me, he would have done that too.

The doorbell rang and startled me. It was Dr. Gray. Two hours had passed. I gathered myself and locked up those raw emotions. It was rare that I allowed them to resurface because they were much too painful. However, whenever I needed to unlock, John was always there to cradle me.

But now he wasn't.

I let Dr. Gray in, but I was having a hard time focusing my attention on the reality of my darkness. I would have preferred to continue daydreaming about my John and our baby boy.

At any rate, Dr. Gray was very careful with his choice of words. I think he was trying to gauge my emotional stability. I assured him I had accepted the fact that John's accident probably could not have been prevented. That's when he delivered the mindboggling blow to my heart.

"I don't think this was an accident. I suspect there was foul play involved. Some of the prisoners and guards had been talking amongst themselves, trying to figure out how to stop John from spreading the Gospel Message!"

I broke out in a cold sweat. My body started shutting

down with every belabored breath I took. Losing John due to an accidental slip and fall was one thing. If I lost him due to premeditated foul play, that was something I would never be able to accept.

With every ounce of my remaining strength, I took a deep breath and asked, "Foul play? What makes you think that, Dr. Gray?"

He went on to explain conversations he'd had with John about that very topic. While he reached many and ushered them into their own personal relationships with their Savior, not everyone at the prison welcomed the Gospel. Some wanted him to stop. John was keenly aware of what he faced; yet he decided to quietly continue what he had considered his prison ministry.

He even likened himself to John the Baptist, who was beheaded in prison. He told me about one night during his Bible study time, he was reading the book of Mark. Chapter 6 tells the story of how King Herod summoned an executioner to prison and ordered him to bring John's head back to him on a platter. He never thought in a million years that he would be in any real danger though. He said he was "John the Batista" and hoped he would not suffer the same agonizing fate as John the Baptist for spreading the Gospel.

Dr. Gray said he often reminded him to watch his surroundings and to be careful who he chose to share the Gospel Message with. Not everyone would become a believer, and regardless of how much he wanted to see all those men come into covenant relationship with Jesus, it was not going to happen. It didn't happen when Jesus himself walked the earth.

"Elizabeth, you do know that John and I became friends. When my official time with him ended and no additional visits were approved by the warden, I continued visiting him on my own time. I came to love John as a dear brother, so I share your grief today."

Of course John had shared that information with me. He was so thankful to be able to count Dr. Gray as a true friend whom he felt would stick by him even closer than a brother. I had not even thought about that. Dr. Gray was grief-struck. He did not come to visit me on behalf of the prison. He was visiting on behalf of his friendship with John.

I needed a psychologist myself at that moment. I teetered between emotions too numerous to count: grief, shock, agony, sadness, disappointment, heartache, pain, disgust, anger, hate, sorrow, despair, emptiness, misery, depression, and lament to name a few.

The gut-wrenching news that they had not been able to save John was hard enough to accept. I asked Dr. Gray how in the world would I be able to withstand this news of his death being purposeful, if it indeed proved to be true.

"By grace, Elizabeth. That's how you will deal with this—by God's grace."

Dr. Gray reached his hand toward me and asked if we could pray. I held his hand, but all I could mumble was, "God, help me!"

He asked me to focus on 2 Corinthians 12:9, which says, "And he said unto me, my grace is sufficient for thee: for my strength is made perfect in weakness. Most gladly therefore will I rather glory in my infirmities, that the power of Christ may rest upon me."

Then he prayed:

"Dear God of all sufficient grace. As we look to you in our time of sorrow, we ask that you deliver us so that we may glorify you. From where we are standing right now, we don't see how our dear John's death and this overwhelming grief we are feeling glorifies you. We are praying out of obedience and faith in your word. May your power shine brightly in our incredible time of loss and weakness. We need healing, comfort, and peace. We need your grace, the grace you promised is enough for whatever we may need. Our need today is great. We ask that you be glorified in our lives as we mourn our insuperable loss, yet walk in faith. In Jesus' name, amen."

That prayer brought such comfort. God's grace was sufficient!

Chapter 23

Flying Solo

It didn't matter what the Prisons and Probation Ombudsman investigation proved. Whatever the final outcome, it would not bring John back. I trusted that the system would work, and if foul play caused my husband's death, I wanted all those responsible brought to justice. However, I could not dwell on that. I would follow at a distance and prayed that God would reveal the truth.

What was important was giving John a proper burial, which I did. I chose to return home to Tel Aviv and lay my husband's body to rest right next to Matthew. I knew neither of them were in that cold, hard ground. Just as I dreamed, I knew where they were. I saw them walking shoulder-to-shoulder down that street paved with gold toward the light where the Son shined brightly.

How thankful I was that Dr. Gray offered to accompany me to Tel Aviv. He took care of the details of having John's body sent home. On the flight back to London after the burial, I couldn't help but think about the last flight John and I had taken together. Twenty months prior, we had not an inkling of how we would spend our last days together as husband and wife. Thanks to the Gospel Message of John

3:16, I knew without a doubt how we would spend our eternity, though.

Dr. Gray escorted me from the airport back to my condo. As I was getting out of the car, he urged me once again to take some time to figure out what to do next. He said he would be with me every step of the way if I needed his guidance or support. I invited him in for tea because I wasn't prepared to be alone.

While sitting at the kitchen table, he asked me out of the blue, "Elizabeth, did you know that John the Baptist's mother was named Elizabeth? She was the cousin of Mary, the mother of Jesus. Did you also know that Elizabeth was considered to be a righteous woman in the eyes of God, and she was known for her prayerfulness?"

I had no idea. I was still working my way through the New Testament and had a lot to learn. I knew enough, though. John guided me very carefully. If I ever had any questions, all I had to do was refer back to the letter Grace sent him, along with the supplemental material. The warden made sure I had all of my husband's personal belongings from prison, which wasn't much, except the letter. That was all we needed anyway, as it changed our lives for all eternity.

I also had my new church family. The bereavement committee had proven to be a priceless blessing as well. Without them and Dr. Gray, I have no idea how I would have survived those initial dark days all alone.

We sipped our tea. I told Dr. Gray, "I want to pursue a closer walk with Jesus. With no plans for a future that did not include John, I need God's guidance. I want to be known for my prayerfulness too, just like John the Baptist's mother."

"Good!" he said. "Prayer is the key that unlocks the door."

It was getting late, and I was exhausted. He could see it on my face. We finished our tea, and Dr. Gray got up to leave. Like a close family member, he reached to give me a brotherly hug. Expressing his heartfelt sympathy and condolences once again, he asked me to promise that I would call him if I ever needed anything.

"Dr. Gray, I promise!"

He said, "We're family now. Call me Luke."

I breathed a sigh of relief but also one of loneliness after he left.

I prepared for bed, giving no thought as to what my day would be like the following morning. Eventually, I would take care of final business in London, but what next? It was then that I remembered what I told John on one of our early visits.

"As soon as you walk free, we are going to board that flight you never got to take at Heathrow and head to Los Angeles, where we will start our lives all over again."

John was walking free!

I dragged myself up from the kitchen table and made my way to the bedroom. I must have fallen asleep the moment my head hit the pillow.

My dreams were sweet that night. I heard John's voice, but I could not see him. I felt his arms cradling me just as he had done when we lost Matthew. My pillow became John's chest where I nestled.

The sound of a neighbor's security alarm startled me from my deep sleep. As tired as I was, I found it difficult to drift off again, so I began to pray.

Then I prayed some more.

It must have taken at least a couple of hours before I fell asleep again. When the sunlight shining through my curtains woke me up, I felt rejuvenated. Not only was I refreshed, I had my answer.

It was time for me to board that flight John never got to take. My new life without him would begin in Los Angeles. For almost two years, we had planned to move to California. I had a compelling feeling that was God's answer to my prayer. I jumped out of bed and hurried about my day with a smidgen of joy in my shattered heart.

It had been quite some time since I felt like singing. I danced around the room like I did the day we got married, singing *Hava Nagila.* It was the same song I sang to John the day I was able to bring him home from the hospital in Tel Aviv after he suffered the mental collapse.

> *Let's rejoice*
> *Let's rejoice*
> *Let's rejoice and be glad*

My heart was rejoicing. My work was not finished. I would carry on in John's memory and honor. He would be proud of me. I would forever be Mrs. John Batista, and nothing made me prouder than to continue the legacy he started in prison. How ridiculous that must sound, to be proud of the work my husband did while incarcerated, but what he did had eternal consequences.

God's redemption of my husband's soul helped to heal my soul deep within in ways I thought not possible.

Although my heart was broken with a void never to be filled, I preferred that over never feeling John's love for me. I would have to find the strength to continue my journey without him. It was hard enough when we lost our baby, but at least I had John's strong shoulder to lean and cry on. Now I had no one except my faith. No one except Jesus.

Somehow, Jesus was enough.

It took a couple of weeks for me to finalize things in London. When I left, the report from the investigation had not been submitted. They assured me they would keep me apprised. I trusted they would but didn't care if they did or not. There was nothing they could do or say to bring my dear John back to me. My resolution will not come until I am reunited with him on the other side.

God's grace is sufficient.

I saw Luke one final time before I left London. I told him all about my plans. He was supportive but cautious. His parting words to me were this:

"Elizabeth, you are the wife of John the Batista. Go in peace knowing your life will now revolve around prayer."

The next day, I boarded a plane at Heathrow headed to Los Angeles and settled in at an extended stay hotel until I made more permanent arrangements. I certainly never thought my first trip to America would be a solo flight. Oh, how I longed for John to be by my side like he always was. I never thought I would have to face this world without him. Yet I was able to find comfort knowing he was in eternity, and I would continue the work he began so others could meet him in heaven one day too.

I slowly began getting acclimated to the area and what I would need to do to survive my new life. I wanted the rest of my time on earth to reflect the love and adoration I had for my husband. It was my honor to be his wife. I wanted others to discover the same grace he discovered in the most unlikely manner.

Three weeks after arriving in LA, I knocked on Grace's door.

"Hello, Mrs. Williams. I'm Elizabeth Batista, John's wife. I'm here to help you spread the Gospel Message of John 3:16 around the globe."

Tears filled her eyes.

And we, two forever connected widows, embraced.

Afterword

The Gospel Symbol
Written by Terry Gurley

Let's take a look at each part of John 3:16 and show how the Gospel Symbol reflects its meaning in picture form.

For God so loved the world that he gave his one and only Son, that whoever believes in him shall not perish but have eternal life. John 3:16

For God so loved the world that he gave his one and only Son . . . God gave his son, the second member of the Trinity, as a sacrifice for the sin of the world. God the Son is making a blood covenant with God the Father for the sons and daughters of Adam on the cross. The blood of God and the blood of man ran through the veins of Jesus. He is the only man who can take away sin. The Gospel Symbol uses the three crosses to illustrate this point.

That whoever believes in him . . . believes what? That the integrity of Jesus is true in this blood covenant with the Father. Jesus paid the debt for our sin, and his death was required for the sin-debt of mankind. The Gospel Symbol uses the sign of covenant, the path of blood, to symbolize the covenant between the Father and Son for us.

Shall not perish . . . The word "perish" points to a soul absent of forgiveness and outside of the blood covenant between the Father and the Son. This soul is condemned to eternal death, separated from God forever. But the soul that has been brought into the covenant is in Christ Jesus. The sin that causes eternal death and separation is no longer a destination because there is no condemnation for the ones in Christ Jesus. To leave the body, as we all will one day, is to be in the presence of God completely forgiven. The blood of Jesus covers all sin. So, the Gospel Symbol uses a stone pulled away from an empty tomb to symbolize Jesus conquering death.

But have eternal life . . . the future of the covenant believer is to be in the presence of God for all eternity. Jesus is returning with the voice of an angel and the trumpet of God. This angel wing and trumpet is the final component in the Gospel Symbol. The God who created us invites us into this relationship with him. The Spirit of God draws those who respond to this invitation. Jesus would tell people, "Follow me," and if they did, their lives would change. A changed life is what we can expect as we walk with Jesus. Jesus paid the price for sin so anyone may receive his Spirit. Jesus promised he would never leave us and nothing could remove us from him after we have been brought into his covenant.

Critical Information

The most important message God has ever given to the people of the world is the Gospel of Jesus Christ. Because in him, and only him, we can be in relationship with God.

"Jesus said to him, I am the way, and the truth, and the life. No one comes to the Father except through me" (John 14:6).

What is this Gospel of Jesus Christ?

The information breaks into four parts:
1. A savior is *promised.*
2. He *died* a substitutionary death for all sins on a cross.
3. He *rose* from the grave on the third day and ascended to heaven.
4. He promised to *return* for his believers one day in the future.

1. *A savior is promised* (thus defining what kind of relationship we are invited into by God) visually represented by the sideways 8, the path of blood in a covenant relationship: "When the sun had set and darkness had fallen, a smoking fire pot with a blazing torch appeared and passed between the pieces. On that day the Lord made a covenant with Abram" (Gen. 15:17–18).

2. He died a substitutionary death for all sins on a cross visually represented by the cross: "How that Christ died for our sins according to the scriptures" (1 Cor. 15:3).

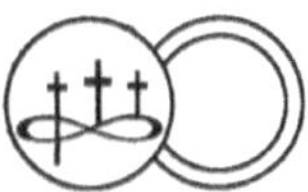

3. He rose from the grave on the third day and ascended to heaven visually represented by the stone rolled to the side of an empty tomb: "That he was buried, that he was raised on the third day according to the Scriptures" (1 Cor. 15:4).

4. He promised to return for His believers one day in the future visually represented by the angel wing and trumpet. "For the Lord himself will descend from heaven with a shout, with the voice of *the* archangel and with the trumpet of God, and the dead in Christ will rise first" (1 Thess. 4:16).

So even more simply phrased, he was *promised,* he *died,* he *rose,* and he is *coming back.*

Jesus left the planet forty days after being resurrected from the grave. He ascended into the clouds as his disciples watched from a place in Israel known as the Mount of Olives. He spoke his last words to them as a command in Matthew 28:16–20: "Then the eleven disciples went to Galilee, to the mountain where Jesus had told them to go. When they saw him, they worshiped him; but some doubted. Then Jesus came to them and said, 'All authority in heaven and on earth has been given to me. *Therefore go and make disciples* of all nations, baptizing them in the name of the Father and of the Son and of the Holy Spirit, and teaching them to obey everything I have commanded you. And surely I am with you always, to the very end of the age.'"

One becomes a disciple of Jesus Christ by first coming into relationship with God. This *"coming into relationship with God"* is understood by the explanation of his Gospel. Jesus said he is the only way into this relationship with his Father. In order to understand the meaning of Jesus being the only way into this relationship with God, let's look at the first part of his Gospel.

The Promise

This promise of relationship is offered to mankind in the form of an invitation. Reading throughout scripture, this unmistakable invitation was revealed to many in biblical times. Although, one man stands out above the rest.

The setting is centuries ago in the Middle East. God speaks to a man named Abram. Instructing Abram to count the stars in the sky, God assures Abram's descendants will outnumber as many stars as he can count. Abram asks God to give him some sort of sign to help him believe, since he and his wife are in their nineties and have no children.

God gives Abram a sign of promise that the people of that day would clearly understand. It is in the form of the strongest handshake or contract known to the people of that time. It was a contract known as a *blood covenant.*

The contract was the way men would show their greatest integrity when making a deal. This contract put their very life on the line. The process of a blood covenant had many parts, but God directed Abram to prepare for the final part. This is where the two making the contract would take an animal and cut it into two halves. The two men would then stand in the blood between the split animal. They would join hands and state the terms of the agreement. The implications were, *"If we break this agreement, may God do to us what we just did to this animal and to everyone else the covenant would include.*"

Next, the two men would walk the *path of blood,* which was the signing of the contract. They would walk in the blood between the animal halves and then turn around and walk back through the blood, stamping out a figure 8 path between the two pieces on the ground. The symbolism was this: the blood of the animal being the ink, the feet of the two men being the instrument of writing, and the ground being the contract parchment the signatures were recorded onto. After this path was completed, the deal was considered done. The contract was permanent. It could never be broken. Binding one's self with a curse was considered one of the strongest assurances that the covenant would be fulfilled. For another reference in the Bible of binding oneself with a curse, see Jeremiah 34:18–20.

God validates this ritual by telling Abram to cut three animals in half— a cow, goat, and sheep—along with two birds, a turtledove and a young pigeon, which were not cut in half. Each being three years old, the large animals created an awful, bloody mess after the slaughter. Genesis 15:9–10 says, "So he said to him, 'Bring me a three year old heifer, and a three year old female goat, and a three year old ram, and a turtledove, and a young pigeon.' Then he brought all these to him and cut them in two, and laid each half opposite the other; but he did not cut the birds."

Next, birds of prey came and tried to devour the carcasses. Abram drove them away, fighting them off all day. "The birds of prey came down upon the carcasses, and Abram drove them away" (Gen. 15:11).

As the sun sets, Abram falls into a deep sleep. Next, a horrible darkness falls and Abram sees three items appear in the darkness, a container of hot coals, smoke, and a flaming torch. The three items pass between the split animals and the Bible says on that day, God cut a covenant with Abram. "It came about when the sun had set, that it was very dark, and behold, there appeared a smoking oven and a flaming torch which passed between these pieces. On that day the Lord made a covenant with Abram" (Gen. 15:18).

There is an obvious difference with the making of this covenant. The two parties, Abram and God, are not walking through the blood hand in hand as was the normal practice. Abram is not invited to walk in the blood with God since both participants required matching integrity. Abram's integrity could not match God's integrity. God solves the problem of Abram's lack of perfection by walking in his place. Abram sat this one out and only watched God walk in blood for him.

Notice there are three items passing over the blood between the split animals. God shows himself in Abram's vision as three items, which is the Trinity represented. One of the three items is representative of the pre-incarnate Jesus Christ, the second member of the Trinity. This is God the Son standing in the place for Abram. Walking in the covenant path of blood, God the Son stands in the place so a human could be in covenant relationship with God. This is the one part of the Trinity, God the Son, who would become human, come to earth through the birth of a virgin, and give his life so all people could be baptized into his death, resulting in a relationship with God. This is God the Son, standing in the place for sinners.

This is a very clear picture of what we are invited into with God. The invitation from God is into a covenant positional relationship in him. This covenant relationship with him, which is in him, is secured on *his integrity* and *his work alone.*

Explanation of 888 and the Symbol 8

Let us use the path of blood to represent the *promise of positional relationship,* since this is the procedure God used to show Abram what he was bringing him into and how.

Numbers have meaning in the Holy Scriptures. All letters in Greek and in Hebrew not only have phonic sounds but also have a numeric value. Individual numbers also represent different meanings. The number 1 represents beginnings and eternal God. In the book of Revelation, the list of events numbering 7 is almost uncountable. Interestingly enough, the number 8 represents new beginnings and *salvation.* Also, the Greek letters of the name of Jesus, I H Σ O Υ Σ (iota, eta, sigma, omicron, upsilon, sigma), when their numeric value is added together, have an amazing sum. The values of each letter are as follows: iota, 10; eta, 8; sigma, 200; omicron, 70; upsilon, 400; sigma, 200. The sum of 10 + 8 + 200 + 70 + 400 + 200 is 888. This is interesting because it is three numeric values, which represent salvation, and three numbers that are the path of a covenant promise within the name of the Son of God. Since it was God who made the covenant with Abram, it stands to reason that the Father and Son and Holy Spirit would be represented in the number.

This information helps put the mystery of the Trinity in a more understandable form. The number 888 is one number with three place values with a visual understandable symbol 8, the sign of covenant, which is inviting us into a relationship with God the Father, Son, and Holy Spirit.

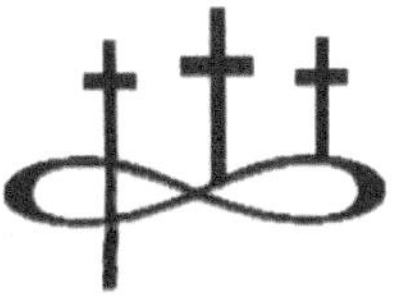

His Death

God the Son, as the second person of the Trinity, walked in blood pledging his life as a ransom for all of mankind that day. He took all the responsibility on himself for what would take care of Abram's lack of integrity along with yours and mine. In the Bible, it is stated that the price of sin is death (Rom. 6:23).

If Abram had walked in the blood with God, he would have died because his integrity could not keep God's requirement of sinlessness. Both parties must have matching integrity, and God's integrity is perfect, and Abram's was not. Nor is yours or mine. As the pre-incarnate Christ, Jesus, the Son of God, walked in Abram's place, he performed this walk in man's place; God the Son was sentencing himself to a death, which is the payment for sin. This payment would purchase a place of right standing before a Holy God for eternity. And since death and sin held humans captive, Jesus Christ, God the Son, became human. This human death would happen centuries later on a cross in Jerusalem, Israel.

God the Son, Jesus, was born just as the Bible had predicted and lived a life sinless before men and God the Father. He was the perfect sacrifice. He is the Lamb of God. He was delivered to the Romans by the Jews and was crucified between two criminals. He died on a cross just as the scriptures had predicted. He became the sinless sacrifice, and his life's blood was given as a ransom for the redemption of all mankind. By giving his life's blood, he completed the process shown to Abram centuries before as he passed over the blood of the covenant animals.

There is now a place in Christ that is redeemed from the death of sin. This place is offered as a position in him. There is now an invitation from God to be *alive in Christ*.

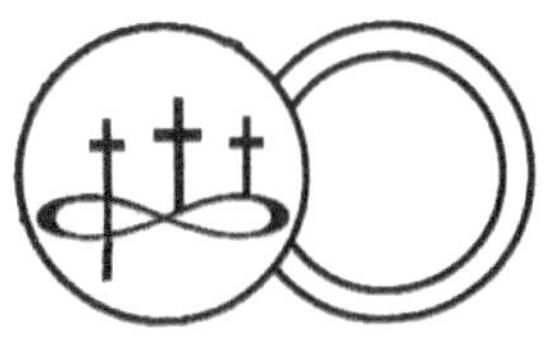

His Resurrection

Just as Jesus said, he would be crucified and raised from the dead on the third day.

Matthew 16:12 tells us, "From that time forth, Jesus began to show unto his disciples how he must go unto Jerusalem and suffer many things of the elders and chief priests and scribes, and be killed and be raised again the third day."

Death could not keep him in the grave!

The gravestone rolled away from his grave three days after he was crucified, and Jesus came out alive, risen from the dead.

Luke 24:1–3 says, "On the first day of the week, very early in the morning, the women came to the tomb, bringing the spices they had prepared. They found the stone rolled away from the tomb, but when they entered, they did not find the body of the Lord Jesus."

This position of covenant relationship in him also gives his covenant believers this victory over death and life everlasting in him.

Covenant believers need not fear death. To be absent from the body is to be present with the Lord. Because of this, death has no victory for the ones that have been brought into Christ. One of the earthly evidences of one being in this covenant relationship is a constant redirection of one's will or behavior. The covenant believer has passed from this present world into an intimate relationship with a living Lord. When one experiences this passing away of the old, dead position of flesh into a living, alive Christ reality, there is a change of awareness.

This awareness is that you are an eternal being created in the image of God and have been placed inside a positional relationship with Christ. This relationship is free from a destination of eternal judgment into a relationship of eternal worship to the Christ. This begins now and carries on into eternity.

His Return

With the voice of an archangel and the trumpet of God.
—1 Thessalonians 4:16

JESUS WILL RETURN!

For the ones who are in covenant with him, there is a great *next event* on the calendar of God, which is the coming of Jesus, in the air, for his covenant believers.

At some point in time, known only to God, in the twinkling of an eye, the trumpet of God will sound, the dead in Christ shall be raised first, and we who are living will be changed in a flash! We all will then be caught up together to meet him in the air (1 Thess. 4:16).

He will take us to be with him to a place that he is preparing for us right now: "And if I go and prepare a place for you, I will come back and take you to be with me that you also may be where I am" (John 14:3).

There we will worship him forever! "And so shall we ever be with the Lord!" AMEN!

On the day Jesus was crucified, there were two men suffering on crosses next to him. One of the men cried out to Jesus and asked to be remembered when he came into his kingdom. Jesus told that man, "Today you will be in paradise with me" (Luke 23:43).

The other man also asked to be saved but only from the situation of being crucified. He mockingly told Jesus to save himself if he were really the Christ and then continued by asking the Son of God to deliver him of the pain of the crucifixion. There is no mention of this man after this.

It is interesting to think that the opposite of love is not hate, but rather separation. Love is relationship. So, on this premise, the opposite of love is aloneness. This seems to have merit since for three of the six hours Jesus hung dying on the cross while there was a horrible darkness like in Abram's vision, he screamed to the Father asking why he had been forsaken. This was Jesus experiencing distance from the Father for the first time in eternity. He had taken on what separates man from God—man's sin—for us. Very much noteworthy is that Jesus was not separated from the Father like sin has done to mankind. Sin is not greater than God.

We can conclude that there are two positions a human's soul can reside. Alone in sin, which is separated and condemned before a Holy God. Or in Christ, which is in covenant with God and seen as righteous after being baptized into his death. Every person can be redeemed through the life's blood of the Son of God, Jesus. All are invited into this relationship without exception. We escape the penalty of sin and separation from God by being in covenant in Christ Jesus. We can be reborn into a right standing position before a Holy God in Christ Jesus. This is what his covenant offers all people.

Like the man dying on the cross beside Jesus, one can ask to be remembered. He offers to bring you into covenant relationship with God through repentance and the baptism of his death.

As one in covenant with God through Jesus Christ, one is now a new creation. The old has gone, the new is here! Now what is ahead is discipleship. Discipleship is a relationship where two or more meet to dig deeper into the Word: studying it, understanding it, living it, and then sharing it. Jesus calls us to be his disciples. One of the most helpful realities in the believer's life is to know he has many new positional responsibilities in this relationship with God.

One of those responsibilities is to share this good news that Jesus invites people into a covenant relationship. The Gospel Symbol is an excellent tool to assist in this adventure.

Our Plans for Spreading The Gospel Message

To create anything that sustains into the minds of people more than a few minutes is a challenge. To create something that is important enough to sustain into the future for more than a thousand years, well, that's the bull's eye on many a thinkers' dartboard. And when someone uncovers from the mines of thought a jewel that resembles a diamond of this value, he hides it away until it can be marketed and capitalized upon. I, my friends, have been given such a diamond. It was given to me not to capitalize upon but rather to give away. I invite everyone to use this language font symbol, much like a writer uses letters to construct the magic of poetry.

The purpose of this symbol is to simplify the four components of the good news of Jesus Christ. They are as follows: God promised to become human, die for the sins of the world, raise from the dead, and return for his believers.

This is one of the ways I am using the symbol to carry out its purpose. I have created a sculpture of an open Bible with this symbol stretched across the open pages with a verse. The verse from this book which best illustrates this message is John 3:16.

I am producing a rubber mold for this concrete sculpture. Churches are primarily sending these molds to missionaries all around the world. These missionaries will produce and place these concrete monuments all around the world until Jesus comes back. My dream is there will be hundreds of thousands of these teaching tools on the planet available to instruct people that come through the Great Tribulation. Evangelism will be a part of what we do during the Millennium Kingdom of Christ, and different languages will still be a challenge. This picture of the Gospel of Christ will be useful.

When you as a covenant believer come back with Christ to rule with him during his Millennium Kingdom, what will be here on earth to show that you were here engaged in the work of sharing the Gospel? If you have no answer, then I invite you to be part of using this ministry of *giving the rocks voice.*

You can contact us through our website: http://www.john316globalplacement.com

Jesus commands his covenant believers to share this good news with the world. God became man, died for the sins of the world, rose from the dead, and is coming back for his believers. I invite you to use this tool, this picture that illustrates these four points of the greatest news God has ever commanded you to share.

If you would like to be part of the placement of this sculpture around the world, I would love to share how you can be a part. Our method is simple. This concrete sculpture is made from a rubber mold. Churches and individuals are sending the molds all around the world so that like-minded Gospel-sharing brothers and sisters will make and place the sculptures around their area. Imagine this tool assisting with sharing the Gospel all around the world in every language.

Remember, pictures are the universal language system. Everyone understands a picture in his or her own language.

I believe God is going to lead as we saturate the planet with these monuments before he returns. I have expectations of these monuments being here sharing the Gospel throughout the Tribulation into the Millennium Kingdom. These concrete sculptures last a very long time, and since concrete only gets harder, we can expect them to be here for hundreds of years. When we are here with our Lord Christ Jesus during his thousand-year reign on earth, imagine the joy of seeing something here that says, "I was here once, and I made effort to share the good news of my Lord." And since the sharing of the Gospel will be part of the millennium kingdom, this concrete tool will still be in service.

My invitation for you to saturate the globe with this open Bible with the Gospel in the universal language system on the open pages is my desire. The sun is setting, and we must work while there is light. The world is very large, but we still have a postal system that takes packages all around the world. Let's do this!!!

~ Terry Gurley, Principle Director/Creator of *The Gospel Symbol*

"For by grace are ye saved through faith; and that not
of yourselves; it is the gift of God."
(Ephesians 2:8 KJV)

~

"For God so loved the world that he gave his one and
only Son, that whoever believes in him shall not
perish but have eternal life."
(John 3:16 NIV)

www.ingramcontent.com/pod-product-compliance
Lightning Source LLC
Chambersburg PA
CBHW031409310726

48971CB00003B/789